**"Please, Je
Don't tear**

"Why? Would yo_____
songs on Sundays_____
month? It's an old building, Beth."

"It was my mother's church." She bit down
on her bottom lip and shrugged. "Don't you
feel it, Jeremy? After all these years, don't
you feel it?"

Man, she was able to set him on his heels
the way no other woman ever had. Because,
yeah, he felt it. He felt the past. He felt God.
He felt faith. It hit him every single time he
walked in this building. He felt hundreds of
prayers that had been said, probably most of
them for him, his little sister and his mother.

But all of those good memories got lost, tied
up with the bad.

"Sorry, Beth."

He turned and walked away, knowing there
would be tears streaking down her cheeks,
knowing she'd nearly collapse with sadness
and frustration over his stubbornness.

And he also knew that she'd understand
why he was doing this.

Books by Brenda Minton

Love Inspired

Trusting Him
His Little Cowgirl
A Cowboy's Heart
The Cowboy Next Door
Rekindled Hearts
Blessings of the Season
 "The Christmas Letter"
Jenna's Cowboy Hero
The Cowboy's Courtship
The Cowboy's Sweetheart
Thanksgiving Groom
The Cowboy's Family
The Cowboy's Homecoming

BRENDA MINTON

started creating stories to entertain herself during hour-long rides on the school bus. In high school she wrote romance novels to entertain her friends. The dream grew and so did her aspirations to become an author. She started with notebooks, handwritten manuscripts and characters that refused to go away until their stories were told. Eventually she put away the pen and paper and got down to business with the computer. The journey took a few years, with some encouragement and rejection along the way—as well as a lot of stubbornness on her part. In 2006 her dream to write for Love Inspired came true. Brenda lives in the rural Ozarks with her husband, three kids and an abundance of cats and dogs. She enjoys a chaotic life that she wouldn't trade for anything—except, on occasion, a beach house in Texas. You can stop by and visit at her website, www.brendaminton.net.

The Cowboy's Homecoming

Brenda Minton

*Love*Inspired

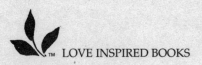

LOVE INSPIRED BOOKS

Recycling programs
for this product may
not exist in your area.

ISBN-13: 978-0-373-87676-1

THE COWBOY'S HOMECOMING

Copyright © 2011 by Brenda Minton

www.LoveInspiredBooks.com

Printed in U.S.A.

He that dwelleth in the secret place of the most
High shall abide under the shadow of the Almighty.
I will say of the Lord, He is my refuge
and my fortress: my God; in Him will I trust.
—*Psalm* 91

This book is dedicated to all of the strong women out there, and to the women wanting to be strong, that they find their strength.

Chapter One

People were never who or what you thought. That's a lesson Beth Bradshaw knew from experience and she had the scars to prove it.

She had even learned things about herself that took her by surprise. Like the fact that she could be strong. She didn't always have to do what pleased others. Sometimes she did what pleased her.

The fact that she was the person sitting on a horse in front of Back Street Church, determined to talk Jeremy Hightree out of his plans for the building was a big moment for her. It was a mountain climbed. It was a fear tackled.

Someone had to do it. So, shaking in her boots, remembering the last time she was here, she sat and contemplated the confrontation.

The horse beneath her shifted, restless from standing. She waved at flies buzzing the animal's neck and ears but her gaze remained on the run-down church in front of her. Things changed, that was part of life. She'd obviously changed since the years spent attending this little church with her mother.

Jeremy Hightree had changed. She knew he'd changed because only huge changes could bring him back to Dawson, Oklahoma, with the plans he had for this building.

The church had been untouched and neglected for too many years. The lawn had grown into a field of weeds. The exterior had faded from white to gray and the paint was chipped and flaking off. After one hundred years of service, the tiny church with the tall steeple had become a forgotten piece of the past.

So why should she care what Jeremy planned on doing to a forgotten piece of Dawson history? The question rolled through her mind as she dropped to the ground and led the chestnut gelding up the sidewalk, metal hooves clip-clopping on concrete. She looped the leather reins around the handrail and walked up the crumbling concrete steps to the porch. The door stood wide open but she didn't go in. She glanced around, looking for Jeremy, her heart hammering a chaotic rhythm, afraid she'd see him. Afraid she wouldn't.

But this wasn't about seeing Jeremy. Her heart did a funny skip forward, asking her to rethink that last thought. But she wouldn't. She couldn't. This had to be about the church, not schoolgirl emotions.

She took a hesitant step inside the church. It took her eyes a minute to adjust to the dim interior. Filtered light from the dirty stained-glass windows caught dust particles that floated in the air. A bird glided through the building and landed on the pulpit. Her great-grandfather had made that pulpit. The wood was hickory and the stain was natural and light. A cross had been carved into the front.

Her history in this town was tied to this church. And

she had ignored it. She took a deep breath, breathing in dust and aging wood. For a minute she was eight years old again and unscarred, still smiling, still believing in fairy tales and happy endings.

Jeremy was still the little boy who pulled at the ribbons on her new dress and teased her about the freckles on her nose.

But she wasn't eight. She was twenty-eight. Her mother had been dead for eighteen years. And Jeremy wasn't a little boy. He was the man who planned on destroying this church.

Eighteen years of pain tangled inside, keeping her feet planted in the vestibule. The little room where they'd once hung their coats was now draped in spiders' webs, and mice ran from corner to corner. The old guestbook still rested on the shelf where it had been placed years ago. She flipped through the pages and stopped when she got to her name written in a child's penmanship. She remembered her mom standing behind her, smiling as Beth scrawled her name, proud that she'd learned to sign it in cursive.

Too many memories. She didn't need all of them, she just needed to know the truth. If it was true, she would find a way to stop him. She walked down the aisle of the church, her booted feet echoing in the tall ceilinged building. She stopped and waited for everything to settle, for the memories to stop tugging at her. In this memory, her mom was next to her, singing. The piano rocked to a Southern gospel hymn. And behind her...

"Bethlehem Bradshaw, I'll tell on you."

His voice was soft in the quiet sanctuary. She turned, amazed that he could still unsettle her. He stood in the doorway, sunlight behind him, his face in shadows. She didn't need to see his face to know him. She knew that he had short, light brown hair and eyes the color of caramel toffee. She knew his smile, that it turned the left side of his mouth more than the right and always flashed white teeth. He walked with a swagger, his jeans hanging low on his hips and his T-shirt stretched tight across the shoulders of a man.

He was no longer a boy. He was lethal and dangerous. He had plans to destroy something that she wanted to protect.

"Why would you do this?" She hated that her voice shook. She despised that she wanted to run out the back door. The closer he got, the harder it was to breathe, to stand her ground.

She wanted to pound her fists against him and beg him to stop, to leave town and forget this church and whatever he had against the people of Dawson. Instead she stood, frozen, unable to do any of those things. Weak. She hated being weak. And afraid.

"Why would I do what? Tease you?" Jeremy Hightree stopped at the second pew from the front of the church, the one where she'd sat with her mother so many years ago. He leaned against it, hip against the side of the wooden bench.

He had always teased her, she wanted to remind him. He would sit behind her and pull ribbons from her hair. He'd once dropped a plastic spider in her lap during Sunday school.

And he had picked a ragged bouquet of wildflowers the day of her mother's funeral and pushed them into Beth's hands as she walked out the doors of the church with her brother Jason and her father. His brown eyes had been rimmed with red from crying and she had wanted to hug him because her mother had always hugged him.

Her mother had defended him. He was the son of her best friend from grade school. Other people had called him a dirty mess. Her mom had called him a little prince.

Beth's feelings had fallen somewhere in between.

She stepped down off the stage, closer to him. One thing was for certain, he wasn't the dirty little boy anymore. He was a man who had traveled. He had won two world championships; one in bull riding and another in team roping. Little girls had posters of him in their bedrooms and little boys wanted to be him when they grew up.

He'd built a business from nothing.

So why this? Why now? It took a few minutes to gather her thoughts, to know how to respond to him. She needed the right words, the right emotions.

"Why the church, Jeremy? You could buy any piece of land you wanted. You could leave the church and never think about it."

One shoulder lifted in indifference. Instead his gaze shot away from her and his jaw clenched. He was anything but indifferent.

"Let's talk about something other than this church. Funny how people have neglected it for years and now everyone wants to talk about it. It was a public auction, Beth. Anyone could have bought it. I was the only one who showed up to bid."

"I know. I guess we all thought someone else would take care of it." She hated admitting that to him and then begging him to let go of his plans.

He moved a few steps closer and Beth stood her ground. She didn't back away. She wouldn't let him get to her. And he could. She shivered and remembered. The memory was soft, sweet, jagged with emotion.

It was the briefest moment, the briefest memory. Yet she'd never forgotten. They had as much history as this church. They'd grown up together. They'd shared a childhood.

"I'm sorry how things turned out with Chance." His voice changed, got a little rougher, a little less velvet than before.

"You couldn't have known." No one would have guessed the abuse Chance was capable of. But it was over. The divorce had been finalized fifteen months ago.

Jeremy must have known something. He had tried to warn her what Chance was like. The day she left town, he'd seen her waiting at the park and he'd tried to tell her. But she had been desperate to escape.

"Beth?" His voice pulled her from the memories, from the darkness, back to the present and the problem at hand.

"I don't want to talk about Chance."

"I understand. And I don't want to talk about the church. It isn't personal, you know. It's a business decision."

"Is it really? It seems personal to me."

He crossed his arms over a muscular chest. "Maybe it is a little personal. I'm tired of this memory and I'm tired of this church standing like a beacon on this hill."

"That's a little drastic, don't you think? This church hasn't been a beacon in a dozen years."

One shoulder lifted again. "I don't know, maybe. But it's my story, not yours."

"This church meant so much to…" She wasn't going to beg him. She breathed deep, willing herself not to cry.

"It meant a lot to your mother."

His tone had changed again. The rough edges were gone. She looked up as he stood straight again and took a few steps in her direction. His steps were slow, calculated.

Had she really thought she could talk him out of this? A shared moment gave her no claim over him. Memories didn't give her a right to assume he would listen. His story in this church mattered to him, not the memory of a kiss they shared a dozen years ago.

"Yes, it did mean a lot to her." But Beth had only been inside the building a handful of times since her mother's funeral. Eighteen years. After her mother's death her father had caught her here once and dragged her home.

Jeremy watched her. His smile faded a little. His eyes narrowed as he stared hard. His Native American heritage was evident in the smooth planes of his face, tanned a deep brown from working outside. But almost everyone in Dawson shared that heritage, that ancestry. Redheads, blonds, brunettes; hair color and eye color didn't dictate a lack of Native American ancestry. The people of Dawson were proud of that heritage, proud of their strength and resilience.

They were known for bouncing back, for not letting the past get them down.

The past was tied to everything, though. It was the shadow of pain in Jeremy Hightree's eyes. It held her own heart captive. It was the fear that clawed at her chest and woke her up in the middle of the night.

"I'm not sure what to tell you, Beth. Your mom meant a lot to me. But this church is…"

"What? Tell me what this church ever did to you?" She pinned him with a stare, hoping to make him squirm. Instead his expression softened, as if he understood her pain, and was hiding his own behind anger.

She remembered the boy with the bouquet, the one she'd wanted to hug. She couldn't allow herself to compare him to that boy. "Tell me, Jeremy, what will revenge do for you?"

Well, now, the kitten had grown some claws. She stood in front of him, pint-size with dark eyes that flashed fear and fire simultaneously. Her dark brown hair hung in pigtails. She picked that moment to lick lips that trembled. He smiled and for a few minutes he didn't quite know what to say to her, because he was picturing her as a cornered kitten, shaking in her boots but ready to swipe at him. He had a lot of questions for her. He had questions about her life, about Chance Martin, about Dawson.

Instead of asking questions he shook his head and considered walking away. She'd mentioned revenge. He really didn't like that word.

And when she'd said it, his decision didn't feel as good as it had even an hour earlier when he'd stood outside picturing this hill without this church, without the memories that had been chasing him down, biting at his heels.

"It isn't just about revenge." He shrugged and smiled

at Bethlehem Bradshaw. He'd always been a fan of her full name, not the shortened version. The full name had meant something to her mother. And her mother had meant a lot to him. She'd done more for him than people would ever know.

That loyalty struck a raw nerve with him right now. Because Bethlehem's mamma was gone and here was her daughter begging for something that woman would have wanted. She would have wanted this church to remain standing.

But he thought she would have cried at its condition now, because it hadn't been used in years and no one had cared to keep it maintained. She wouldn't have wanted that either.

Of course she would have told him to forgive.

Forgive his mother for being the town drunk. Forgive Tim Cooper for a tiny indiscretion more than thirty years ago and not owning up to it. As far as Jeremy was concerned, Tim Cooper didn't need his forgiveness. That was between Tim and Mrs. Cooper.

Jeremy had a truckload of bad memories. He'd learned early to fight for himself and his little sister. At eight he could make a mean box of mac and cheese. By the time he was ten he could sign his mother's signature on school permission slips. He learned to braid his little sister's hair and wash her clothes.

His sister, Elise, was married now. She and her husband owned a convenience store in Grove. They sold bait to fishermen and coffee mugs to tourists. Elise was big on forgiveness, too.

"It looks a lot like revenge." Bethlehem's soft voice intruded into his memories, shaking him up more than a green Oklahoma sky on a stormy afternoon.

"Bethlehem, I'm not sure what you want me to say."

"Say you won't do this."

"I can't say that." For the first time since he'd bought the church, he had the biggest urge to forget his plans. Because of Beth.

"Why not?"

Jeremy shook his head to clear the thoughts. "I have plans for this piece of property."

He needed a bigger shop for the custom bikes he'd turned from a hobby into a business, an extension of the chain of motorcycle dealerships he owned.

"Do you have plans or are you just angry?"

He leaned in and then he regretted the move that put him a little too close to Bethlehem, close enough to see the flecks of gold in her brown eyes, close enough to get tangled in the soft scent of her perfume.

Man, she was summer sunshine. She was sweet, the way she'd been sweet at sixteen. A guy couldn't forget a kiss stolen along a creek bank on a summer night.

Time to think fast and get the kid he'd been back under the control of the man he now was. And she wasn't making that an easy thing to do.

"Let me ask you a question. How many times have you been to church in the last dozen years or so?"

She turned pink and glanced away from him. "We're not talking about me. And I do go to church."

He smiled at that. "Yeah, we weren't talking about you. But now we are."

Because there was a scar across her brow. It ran into her hairline. A matching scar ran jagged down her arm. She shifted, uneasy, and crossed her arms in front of herself. This church wasn't the only thing he'd like to tear down. If he ever got hold of Chance Martin, he'd probably do the same to him.

But he doubted Chance would ever show his face in Dawson, not if he wanted to live. Because Jeremy figured he probably wasn't the only man in town that wanted to get hold of that coward.

Beth's arms dropped to her sides and she took a few steps toward the door, her eyes shifting from him to the exit. He got that she needed to breathe, and he let her have the space.

At the door she turned to face him again.

"Don't do this. Please." A tear streaked down her cheek.

He let out a sigh and shook his head. "Bethlehem, I'm sorry. I know why this church means something to you. It means something different to me."

"I know and I'm sorry."

"Right."

"I'll buy it from you." She spoke with renewed determination, her dark eyes flashing. "You don't need this land. Do you even plan on staying here?"

"No, I'm not staying here, not full time. I have a home in Tulsa."

"Then don't do it. What will it accomplish? Who do you want to hurt?"

He brushed a hand over the top of his head, over hair cut short, and moved it down to rub the back of his neck.

"I'm done with this conversation, Bethlehem."

"It's a building. It didn't do anything to you."

He looked around, remembering. She was wrong about that. This building tied into a lot of anger. That anger had pushed him to battle it out on the backs of bulls. It had put him on a motorcycle, racing through the desert at speeds that would make most guys wet themselves like little girls.

When he looked at this building, there wasn't a good memory to hang on to. He glanced away from her, away from the second pew where her mother had sat, and he called himself a liar.

Good memories included potluck dinners when he got to sit with Bethlehem and her mother. He had other good memories, like the smile she gave him when she was fifteen and he'd just won a local bull-riding event. She'd smiled and then hurried away with her friends, giggling and shooting glances back at him. Hers had lingered longest and when he'd winked, she'd turned pink and nearly tripped.

"Bethlehem, I am going to tear this church down."

"I feel sorry for you."

"Yeah, lots of people do." But he didn't want her to be one of them.

"I'll do what I can to stop you. I won't let you tear it down."

"What would you do with it, Beth? Open it back up, sing songs on Sundays, serve potluck once a month? It's an old building. It should probably be condemned."

She shrugged and smiled a soft smile. He knew he was in serious trouble then. He got a feeling she was about to pull a one-two punch on him.

She stepped close, her smile pulling him closer.

"Don't you feel it, Jeremy? After all these years, don't you feel it?"

Yeah, he'd seen it coming. No other woman had ever set him on his heels the way she could. Because he knew exactly what she meant and, yeah, he felt it. He felt the past. He felt God. He felt faith. All the things he'd been ignoring and it hit him every single time he walked into this building. He felt hundreds of prayers that had been said, probably most of them for him, his little sister, and his mother.

He remembered Sunday school teachers who had brought him cookies. The pastor back then, Pastor Adkins, and his wife had bought Jeremy and his sister school clothes and Christmas presents.

But all of those good memories got lost, tied up with the bad, when he remembered Tim Cooper on the front pew with his family. Each Sunday they'd showed up in their van, wearing new clothes and happy smiles. When he'd been about six years old there were only a few Cooper kids. As the years went by, the clan grew. The Coopers had about a half dozen kids of their own. They added about a half dozen adopted children.

Jeremy had sat two pews back across the aisle, without a family to have Sunday lunch with, without a dad.

"Sorry, Bethlehem."

He turned and walked away, knowing there would be tears streaking down her cheeks, knowing she'd nearly collapse with sadness and frustration over his stubbornness.

As he walked out the back door his phone rang. He shielded the display and shook his head. He really didn't want to deal with this today. Bethlehem had just about done him in.

But if he didn't answer she'd call again. And again. There was always a crisis in his mother's life.

"Hi, Mom, what do you need?" He held the phone

to his ear and walked across the overgrown lawn to the RV that he'd been living in.

Horse hooves on pavement caught his attention. He turned to watch Bethlehem ride down the road at an easy trot. Her hand came up and he knew she was wiping tears from her eyes.

That made him not much better than Chance Martin.

"Jeremy, this is Carl Duncan." A county deputy on his mom's phone. Great.

"What can I do for you, Carl?"

"I'm sorry to bother you but we've got your mamma down here at the jail. Someone called her in for a disturbance."

"Did she have clothes on this time?" He brushed a hand across his head and looked down at the ground, at his scuffed work boots and at a little black snake slithering a short distance away.

"Yeah, fully clothed but drunk enough we're considering sending her to the E.R."

"Do what you have to do and I'll be there in about thirty minutes."

He slid the phone back into his pocket and turned. His attention landing on the eyesore that used to be Back Street Church. The steeple still stood and a cross reached up, tarnished but intact.

It bothered him, that Bethlehem had made him remember more than he'd wanted to. She'd forced him to recognize other things about this building, this church. She'd made him think about the good things that had happened here.

But it didn't matter. He'd bought this land to raze a church and build a business. He wasn't going to give up on his plans, his dreams, not for Bethlehem or anyone else.

Next week Back Street Church was going to be nothing but a memory.

Chapter Two

The horse flew up the driveway, hooves pounding the ground and neck stretched forward. Beth leaned, reins in her hands, her legs tight around the horse's middle. They flew past the house, past the garden and the barn. She pulled the horse up at the fence and then just sat there on the gelding, both of them breathing hard.

"Take it easy on that colt." The gruff voice didn't lecture, just made a statement.

Beth turned to smile at Lance, her dad's ranch foreman.

"He's barely winded."

"He's needed a good ride, that's for sure. Where you been?"

"Riding." She slid to the ground, the reins still in her hands. Lance took the horse and led the animal to the barn. She followed. The ranch foreman was getting older but he was still burly and fit. He hitched up his jeans with a piece of twine and his shirt was loose over a T-shirt. He glanced back, his weathered face so familiar she wanted to hug him just for being in her life.

"Your daddy has been looking for you. He said he called your phone three times."

"I didn't have a signal."

"The only place in Dawson with a weak cell signal is Back Street." Lance turned, his gray eyes narrowed. "You weren't up at the church, were you?"

"I'm twenty-eight, not twelve."

"I think I know that. I'm just saying, you don't need to mess around up there. And you aren't going to be able to stop Jeremy Hightree from doing what he plans on doing."

"Someone has to stop him."

"Well, the city of Dawson is trying to take care of that. Let them."

"I'm afraid I'm just going to have to help them."

She took the horse's reins from the ranch foreman and led the gelding down the center aisle of the barn. She grabbed a brush off a hook and crosstied the horse. Lance flipped the stirrup over the back of the saddle and loosened the girth strap.

"You can't stop him, Beth. He's got thirty years of mad built up in him."

"He needs to get over it."

"Right, and men always listen when a woman tells them to just 'get over it.'" He said it in a girly voice and shook his head. It was funny, that voice and big old Lance with his craggy, weathered face. Lance had always been there for them. He'd always managed to make her smile. When she was a teenager and thought the world hated her, and she hated it back, Lance had been the one who teased her out of the bad moods.

The horse stomped and Beth ran a hand down the deep red neck. The animal turned and nibbled at her arm before lowering his head to enjoy the loss of the saddle and the feel of the brush across his back.

"I think I'll ride him next weekend in Tulsa."

"He isn't ready for barrels."

She brushed across the horse's back and then down his back legs. "He'll be ready."

"You're as stubborn as your dad. Maybe Jeremy has met his match."

"What about Jeremy?" This voice boomed. The horse jumped a little to the side.

Beth bit down on her bottom lip and then flashed a smile, as if she hadn't been talking about anything important. "Nothing, Dad."

"Right, nothing. I saw you racing up the drive on that horse. Where have you been?"

Her dad walked a little closer. She stood straight, the brush in her hand, and faced him. She'd been backing down all of her life and she couldn't be that person anymore.

"I went to talk to Jeremy Hightree about the church. I have to stop him from tearing it down."

The harsh lines around her dad's mouth softened and he looked away, but not before she saw the sorrow. It still felt like yesterday. Shouldn't it be different? Shouldn't eighteen years soften the pain? She'd been without her mother longer than she'd been with her. There were times that her mother's smile was a vague memory. And more times that she couldn't remember at all.

But her dad missed Elena Bradshaw more than all of them. And missing her meant he disliked Back Street Church as much as Jeremy.

"Dad, she loved that church." Beth had never been brave enough to say it, to put it out in the open. This was the new Beth Bradshaw, the woman who took control. The woman who wasn't afraid. Much.

Her dad raised a hand and turned away, his profile a dark shadow against the bright, outside light. She'd always thought of him as the strongest man in the world. What little girl didn't think that way? As a child she'd tried to match her steps to his. She'd always tried to please him. She had never wanted to hurt him.

"Please, Dad, we have to stop him."

He shook his head and walked out the door, away from her, away from memories. She took a step to follow him, to get him to help. Lance's hand on her arms stopped her.

"Let it go." He released her arm. "Let him have his memories. That church has been empty for years. It isn't all you have of your mom."

"I know it isn't. It's about more than her memory. It's about Jeremy's anger at a building. It's about…" She sighed. It was about her mom.

"Yeah, it's about that building. Everyone in town is talking about it. They all have a reason they think it shouldn't be torn down, Beth. The truth is, they could have done something to save it."

Beth watched her dad walk across the driveway to the house and then she turned to face a man who had been a second father to her. Lance was her mother's second cousin somehow twice removed. He'd taught her to come home strong after the third barrel, to not be afraid as she rushed toward the gate. He'd taught her to rope a calf. He'd taught her to let go of pain. He'd tried to keep her in church, having faith.

"I don't have anything to remember her by, Lance. Everything is boxed up and hidden. Her pictures, her jewelry, and even the quilts she made. He boxed it all up. I don't know if he burned it, gave it away or threw it in the Dumpster."

"He shouldn't have done that. Sometimes a person hurts so bad they don't know what else to do. They box up the pain and I guess your daddy boxed up his memories right along with it."

"She loved that church."

"She sure did. And she loved her family. She'd want those memories unboxed." Lance untied the horse and led him down the aisle of the barn. A horse whinnied from somewhere in the distance. The gelding, Bob, whinnied a reply.

It had been years since Beth thought about the day her dad had started packing everything into boxes. He'd been crazy with grief, pulling pictures off the walls, yanking quilts off beds. Everything that reminded him of Elena Bradshaw had been packed up and hauled off while Beth cried and Jason stoically helped their father.

Lance placed a strong hand on her shoulder.

"I'll feed this horse for you. I think it's about time you talked to Buck about the box she left you. It's yours, Beth. She'd want you to have it." He put the horse in a stall and latched the gate. "And you know this horse isn't ready for Tulsa."

She nodded, still fighting tears, still fighting mad that everyone else always seemed to have answers, to be in control, and she always seemed to be fighting to be strong.

It was a fight she planned to win.

"Yeah, I know."

"Go talk to your dad."

She walked out of the barn and across the dusty driveway toward the house. A lone figure in the garden bent over tomato plants that were just starting to flower. She stopped at the edge of the garden.

"I'm not going to help you save that church." He bent to pick a few weeds.

"I'm not here to talk about the church. I'd like the box my mother left for me." She shoved her hands in her pockets, no longer brave. The deep breath she took did nothing to calm nerves that were strung tight. "If you don't mind."

Her dad turned. He stood straight, his hat tipped back. He was tall and broad, his skin weathered by sun and time but he was still strong.

"What brought that up?" her father asked.

Beth had imagined anger, not a question like that. She didn't really have an answer. "I think it's time. I want to have something to remember Mom by."

"It's just a box of stuff." He shrugged. "I'll bring it down from the attic."

She wanted to rush forward and hug him, but he turned back to the tomato plants. She'd won the battle but it didn't feel like a victory. She whispered "thank you" and her dad nodded. After a few seconds she walked away.

As she entered the house, she remembered the day her mother had sat them down in the living room and explained that she had taken her last treatment. The memory was followed by one of the day they took Elena off life support.

Beth stood in the living room for several minutes and then she walked back out the front door. She pulled keys out of her pocket and headed across the yard to the garage and her truck. It was starting to make sense, why Jeremy would want to do this. Even if she didn't want him to, maybe she understood. Her dad had shoved his pain into boxes and stored them in the attic. She'd run away. Jeremy needed to see that church gone.

As much as she understood, she still planned on finding a way to stop him.

The police station was a long, rectangular building with metal siding that looked more like a forgotten convenience store. In an area like this, they didn't need much for a police station. The occasional robbery, traffic violation or intoxicated driver, those were the extent of the crimes. His mom had probably committed each one, more than once.

Jeremy pulled his truck into a parking space next to a patrol car and he sat there for a long minute because he dreaded going inside. Why had he come back to Dawson? Oh, right, for revenge.

He'd been running from this life for years. He'd done a good job of putting it behind him. He had a successful business building customized motorcycles. He had two world championships. He'd done commercials for cologne and they'd made posters of his ugly mug to sell at rodeo events.

No matter how far he'd gone or what he thought he'd done right, one person knew how to pull him right back into the gutter. A shadow moved in front of the door. On the other side of the glass deputy Carl Duncan waved and motioned him inside.

He'd been fifteen when he bailed Jane out the first time. He'd used his money from lawn jobs and he'd borrowed a car from a neighbor. Back then Carl had been his age, just a kid trying to make a better life for himself. The cop at the time had been Officer Mac. He'd retired years ago.

That was a memory that made him smile. Officer Mac had been a farmer who carried a badge for extra money. When he'd seen Jeremy in that car, he shook his head and told Jeremy he was going to pretend he didn't see an underage driver behind the wheel.

Jeremy pulled the truck keys from the ignition and shoved them into his pocket as he got out of the vehicle. At least he had his own car these days.

He walked across the parking lot, stopping to glance up at the sky, another way to kill time. There were a few dark clouds, nothing major.

Carl pushed the door open. A woman screamed from somewhere at the back of the building. That would be Jeremy's mother. He knew that awful sound and knew that her eyes would be red, her hair a wild mess. They'd been through this more than once.

"What did she do this time?" He grabbed a seat from behind one of the desks and sat down.

"She was in the convenience store trying to convince them you've stolen all of her hard-earned money."

"That would get me a cup of coffee."

They didn't laugh. Carl sat down on the edge of the desk and shrugged. "She's coherent. Sort of."

"Right. So what do I do with her, Carl?"

"Take her home." The cop shrugged. He didn't have answers, either. "Maybe put her in a home. I don't know, Jeremy. I'm real sorry, though."

"Me, too." Jeremy loosened his white cowboy hat and then pushed it back down on his head. "Yeah, maybe a home. She might actually get sober."

"Right, that would be good. She looks a little yellow."

Her liver. He didn't know how it had held up this long.

"Do I owe you anything?" He pulled the wallet out of his back pocket and Carl shook his head.

"No, there weren't any charges. I just brought her in to keep her from doing something crazy. Are you really going through with the church situation?"

It always came back to that. The people in this town ought to be thanking him for getting rid of that eyesore, not questioning his motives. Considering that the church had been one step away from being condemned, he didn't know why everyone had a problem with his plans.

His mother screamed again. "Get me out of here! I didn't break any laws. I'll get a lawyer."

Jeremy laughed, shook his head and stood. "I'd better get her home before she hires a lawyer."

Carl nodded and headed down the narrow hall. He stopped at the farthest door and pulled keys from his pocket. "Mrs. Hightree, I'm letting you out now. Can you settle down for me or do I need to keep you overnight?"

"You can't keep me overnight. I didn't do anything wrong."

"Public intoxication." Carl slid the key in the lock. "Or public nuisance."

He unlocked the door and she stepped out of the room, a pitiful figure in a housedress, gray hair sticking out in all directions and a gaunt face. Her attention quickly turned to Jeremy. She frowned and stomped her foot.

"I'm not going with *him*."

"Mrs. Hightree, you don't have a choice."

She flared her thin nostrils at them and shook her head. "I have choices. I can walk out of here. I can head on home without his help."

Heat crawled up Jeremy's cheeks. After a lifetime of this, a guy should be used to it. It wasn't as if her behavior took people by surprise. What did surprise him was how old she looked, and how bad. He'd seen her less than a week ago and she hadn't looked this old.

She had been a pretty woman twenty years ago. Thirty-one years ago she had obviously turned some heads. He pushed that thought aside because now wasn't the time to get caught in the muck.

"Mom, we're going home."

"Janie, my name is Janie."

He grabbed her arm, loose flesh and bones. "Right, Jane."

He hadn't called her mom since he was ten and he'd found her passed out in the yard when he came home from school. That had been enough to take the word "Mom" right out of his vocabulary.

"You don't have to hold me. I'm not going to run."

"No, but you might fall down."

She wobbled a little, as if to prove his point. "There's nothing wrong with me."

Jeremy shot a look back at Carl. The cop stood behind them, sorry written all over his face. "Thanks, Carl. You're sure there weren't any expenses this time?"

"Not this time. Do you want me to call the hospital in Grove? Maybe she should be seen?"

"I'm fine, I said." She jerked her arm free from his

hand. "I don't need either of you holding me or telling me what to do. I just need to go home."

"I'll take her home." Jeremy opened the door and motioned his mother through. "See you later."

"Yeah, we'll see you around. Maybe we can meet for lunch at the Mad Cow tomorrow?"

"Right, and you can try to talk me out of what you all think is a big mistake." Jeremy smiled, and Carl turned a few shades of red, right to the roots of his straw-colored hair. "I'll meet you for lunch, but if everyone was so worried about this church, why didn't you all do something sooner?"

"Yeah, I guess you've got a point there, Jeremy. Maybe we just thought it would always be there."

"It would have fallen in, Carl."

Carl stood in the doorway while Jeremy held on to his mother to keep her from falling off the sidewalk. "My grandpa goes up there once a month to check on the place. I think a lot of the older people in town would love to have it opened up again, but nobody had the money and the younger families have moved away."

"Call me and we'll talk over burgers at Vera's."

Carl nodded. "I'd appreciate that."

Jeremy escorted his mom out the door and down the sidewalk. She weaved and leaned against him. Tires on pavement drew his attention to the road. Tim Cooper. Yeah, they'd have to face each other sooner or later. They hadn't talked since the day Jeremy learned the truth. The day Tim Cooper wrote him a check, because it was the right thing to do.

Jeremy opened the door on the passenger side of the truck. Jane wobbled and her legs buckled. When he tried to lift her up she swatted at his hands.

It took a few minutes but he got her in the seat and buckled up. They headed down the road, toward Back Street but then turned east. The paved country road led to a tiny trailer surrounded by farmland. It had two bed-rooms and a front porch that was falling in. More than once he'd tried to get her to move. But this was her house and she didn't want his money.

It was the only thing she'd ever owned. This trailer was her legacy. He shook his head as he drove down the road. He thought about how he'd envied the Coopers and their big old ranch house.

His mom choked a little and leaned. Great. Her body went limp and she fell sideways. He eased into the drive-way of the trailer and pulled the emergency brake. He put the windows down and waited while she got sick on the floor of the truck.

Maybe they would head for the hospital. He pulled her back in the seat and wiped her mouth with the hand-kerchief he pulled out of his pocket. "Mom, are you with me?"

She shook her head and mumbled that he was as worthless as his father. Yeah, she was with him. He shifted into reverse and glanced in his rearview window. A blue truck pulled in behind him. Great, what he didn't need was a big dose of sympathy in brown eyes that dragged his heart places he didn't want to go.

But that's what he was about to get.

"Leave me here," his mom mumbled without moving from her prone position on the seat next to him.

"I can't leave you here. You need help."

"Since when do you care?"

"I don't know, since forever, I guess." And he'd

proven it time and again. His mom passed out as Beth rapped on his driver's side window.

Beth shouldn't have stopped but she'd seen Jeremy's truck at the police station. She'd watched in her rearview mirror as he helped his mother down the sidewalk. For a few minutes she'd listened to the smart Beth who insisted she should drive on home and forget it. But the other Beth had insisted she put her heart on the line. And that's why she was looking through the window of his truck into eyes that were slightly lost and a lot angry.

His window slid down. "Imagine seeing you here."

"I thought you might need help."

"No, we're fine. I'm taking her to the hospital."

In the seat next to him his mother made a grunting sound that resembled a negative response. Obviously she didn't want Beth around and she wasn't interested in going to the hospital.

"Do you want me to ride over there with you?" She regretted the words the minute they were out. No one in their right mind would volunteer. But she had gone and done it.

His mother leaned to the floor again. Jeremy groaned and reached in the backseat of the truck for a towel that he tossed on the floor. "You wouldn't happen to have a bag or a bucket in your truck, would you?"

"Give me a sec and I'll check." Beth hurried back to her truck. She pushed through the contents in the toolbox in the bed of her truck and found a small bucket, a roll of paper towels and a spray bottle of window cleaner.

She returned to the passenger side of Jeremy's truck

and opened the door slowly, carefully. Jane Hightree was passed out, leaning toward her son. Beth handed him the bucket and then she sprayed the floor down and covered it with paper towels.

"Beth, you don't have to do this." His voice was quiet and a little tight with emotion. She glanced up as she pulled on leather gloves.

"I don't mind. I'm good at cleaning up messes."

"Yeah, well, I usually clean up my own messes."

She ignored him and cleaned, tossing it all in a bag she'd pulled out from under her truck seat.

"I appreciate the help." Jeremy reached for the passenger seat belt, pulling it around his mother, even though she remained prone on the seat. "I'm going to take her to Grove."

"Do you want me to go?"

He shook his head and then looked up, smiling at Beth. "I can handle this, but thank you." He released the emergency brake and his hand went to the gearshift.

She nodded. "Let me know what happens with your mom."

"I'll do that."

Beth closed the door and walked back to her own truck. As she climbed behind the wheel he backed out of the drive and headed down the highway. Beth went the opposite direction, toward her brother's house because being strong on her own wasn't easy. When she'd confronted Jeremy at Back Street Church she had meant to talk him out of something, not put herself in his life. She had to keep her focus on what was important. The goal wasn't to get tangled up in his life, it was to save the church.

Chapter Three

Beth finished her phone call and sat down at the table with a cup of coffee. After helping Jeremy with his mother the previous evening, she'd had a long talk with her brother Jason about ways to save Back Street Church. Thanks to his wife Alyson they had a very clear idea of how to accomplish their goal. They'd learned that the building had turned 100 the previous year.

They were still digging but it was possible the building could be saved by having it listed on an historical registry. The phone call Beth had made would set the plan in motion.

And she didn't know how she felt about what she'd done. As much as she didn't want the church torn down, she also didn't want to hurt Jeremy.

It seemed that no matter what, someone would get hurt. Either Jeremy or the people in town who cared about the future of the church. He had plans for a business. Beth saw the church as a connection to her mother. Others in town had similar stories and reasons for wanting the building to remain standing.

She took a sip of her coffee and reached for the box sitting on the table in front of her.

Her dad had finally given it to her the previous evening after she'd gotten home from visiting Jason and Alyson. Now that she had it, though, she didn't know what to do with it. She'd left it sitting on her dresser last night, untouched. Thirty minutes ago she had carried it into the kitchen. She'd been staring at it while she ate her cereal and then made the phone call to the historical society.

She let out a shallow, shaky breath and reached for the box. It was just a plain metal box. Her mother had intended for her to have this eighteen years ago. Eighteen long years, with so many mistakes, so much heartache in between.

Would her life have been different if her mother had lived? Would Beth have made different choices, taken a different path? Those were questions that would never have answers.

She lifted the lid of the box and a sob released from deep down in her chest. Tears followed as she lifted her mom's Bible from the box. Her mother's most prized possession. Of course her dad wouldn't have wanted Beth to have that Bible. He would have seen it as the root of all their problems; the same way he blamed Back Street Church for her mother's death.

He had needed to blame something, or someone. He had picked the church Elena turned to when the doctors told her there was nothing they could do.

Beth opened the Bible and stared through tear-filled eyes at her mother's handwritten notes in the margins. Reading those notes, it was as if her mom was there, teaching her about life. There were notes about faith, sermons, and verses that were her favorites.

She closed the Bible and placed it on the table. There were other things in the box. Her mother's wedding ring. A book of devotions. Her journal.

The journal was leather bound. The pages were soft, white paper that had yellowed with time. The writing had faded but was still legible. Beth flipped through the pages. The last half of the journal was blank. But the final entries, pages and pages of entries, were written to Beth.

She skimmed several but paused on the one dated August 5.

Dearest Beth, you're barely ten and I know this isn't going to be easy for you, but I want you to know that I love you and God has a plan for your life. Don't give up. Don't forget that your daddy, even if he's hurting and angry, loves you. And don't hurry growing up. It'll happen all too soon. Love will happen. Life will happen. Don't rush through the days, savor them. Love someone strong.

Love someone strong. Beth closed her eyes. She didn't know if she'd ever really been in love. Chance had been a mistake, an obvious mistake. He'd been her rebellion and a way to escape her father's quiet anger. Now she realized her dad had been more hurt than angry. But at eighteen she hadn't cared, she had just wanted to get away from Dawson and the emptiness of her life.

Her life was no longer about Chance. It couldn't be about what she'd been through. Instead it was about what happened from this day forward.

Jeremy Hightree didn't understand that. He still saw the church as a connection to his troubled childhood.

Maybe her mother's words could change his heart. She put everything back in the box but she didn't replace the lid. She wouldn't do that. It was a silly thing but she couldn't put the lid back on the box. Instead she carried it down the hall to her bedroom and placed the box on her dresser.

She walked out the French doors of her room, onto the patio that was her own private sanctuary. She stood in the midst of her flowers and the wood framed outdoor furniture that blended with the surroundings.

When she came home a short year and a half ago this had been her healing place. She'd planted flowers and she'd hidden back here, away from questions and prying eyes. In this garden no one questioned the jagged cut on her face or the arm that had needed to be reset.

This morning she was escaping from other emotions. Her mother's memory, Jeremy's plans for the church, her own fears.

She really needed to slow down. Everything was coming at her in fast forward. It was time to pray and plan her next move, before she rushed forward and did something she would regret.

At last she had fallen to sleep. Jeremy stood at the door of his mother's room and waited for her to move, to wake up and yell again. She'd done a lot of that since the previous evening when the hospital had transported her to the long-term facility a short distance from Grove, and only five minutes from Dawson.

She'd done so much screaming this morning that the nursing home staff had called him to see if he could calm her down. Surprisingly she had calmed down immediately when she saw him.

He sighed and turned to go.

"Jeremy, how are you?"

Wyatt Johnson walked down the hall. Jeremy shrugged one shoulder and turned his attention back to his mother's room, to the bed, and to the thin figure covered with a white blanket.

"Do you need anything?" The two had gone to school together. They'd ridden horses together and roped calves together. Wyatt's horses and Wyatt's calves. They'd been friends, even though Jeremy hadn't been a part of Wyatt's social circle. They'd traveled to rodeos together and fought their way out of a few corners together.

"No, we don't need anything. It looks as if she'll be here for a while." For the rest of her life. Her liver was damaged from years of alcohol abuse. Her brain wasn't much better.

There must have been a time when she'd been a good person. He really tried to remind himself of that; of the reality that she had fed him and cared for him.

Or he liked to hope she had.

When he thought of gentle touches, it sure wasn't his mother he thought of.

"I'm sorry." Wyatt leaned his shoulder against the doorframe. "Guess there isn't much more a person can say."

"Nope, not much, but thanks." Jeremy turned from the room and headed down the hall, Wyatt Johnson at his side. Jeremy stopped at the nurse's station. The woman behind the desk looked up, her glasses perched on the end of her nose. "I'm leaving."

"We'll call if there are any problems."

"Right." He stood there for a minute, wondering if there was something else he should say or do. The nurse continued to stare at him. She finally lowered her gaze to the papers she'd been reading.

He guessed that was his cue to move on. So he did. Wyatt moved with him. When they got to the door Jeremy punched in the code and pushed the door open.

"Wyatt, I don't want to talk about the church. Not now."

"I hadn't planned on bringing it up."

An alarm sounded. Wyatt reached past him and pulled the door closed. He pushed other buttons on the keypad.

Jeremy stared at the closed door, at his truck in the parking lot and then shifted his attention back to Wyatt. He couldn't be mad at a guy who'd gone through the things Wyatt had gone through; losing his wife, raising two little girls on his own. And then falling in love with a preacher's daughter. At least Wyatt's situation had a decent ending.

The single life was good enough for Jeremy. He dated women who wanted nothing more from him than a decent meal and a dozen roses to end things. That philosophy kept his life from being complicated.

He hadn't seen too many happy relationships in his life and figured he was a lot better off than the friends who'd started believing they needed to settle down and have a family. Wyatt didn't look too worse for wear, though.

"Looks like it might storm." Jeremy nodded toward the southern sky. It was Oklahoma, so there was always a pretty good chance it might storm.

"Yeah, looks that way. We're under a tornado watch

until this evening. No warnings, yet." Wyatt pulled keys out of his pocket.

"Yeah." Jeremy ran out of things to say about the weather.

Wyatt grinned and tipped his hat back. "I know you don't want to talk about the church, but you bought it and you had to know that'd stir up a hornet's nest. I've known you a long time and you've always been fond of a hornet's nest if you could find one."

Jeremy told himself not to respond to his friend's baiting. He smiled and kicked his toe at the ground. Yeah, he wasn't going to ignore it.

"Wyatt, the church was for sale and I bought it. If people in Dawson are suddenly attached to a building they've neglected for years, that's their problem. Someone else could have bought it."

"Someone else could have," Wyatt said. "No one did."

"Right. I bought it and I plan on building a business that might give a few people in Dawson the jobs they need."

"That's a decent idea. But you have two hundred acres across from the church. Why not build your business over there?"

"I'm building a house on that side of the road and I'm buying cattle."

"Yeah, I saw that they finished framing the house yesterday. It's pretty huge for one guy. Are you actually going to live in Dawson?"

Jeremy stopped at the edge of the sidewalk. "I'm going to be here part of the time."

"The church means a lot to a lot of people. I know it doesn't seem that way."

"No, it doesn't and I kind of wonder why everyone suddenly realizes the church means something to them." Jeremy glanced at Wyatt.

"Pastor Adkins kept me in church after my dad's big indiscretion. I guess Back Street is what got me where I am today."

"Gotcha." Jeremy processed the story with the others he had been told. "Sorry, Wyatt, I have to get back and get back to work."

"Work?"

"Business doesn't stop because the boss is out of town." He gave Wyatt a tight smile. "I'm managing my business from a laptop in the RV and trying to help Dane with a flaw in a bike we're designing."

Jeremy had partnered with Dane Scott in team roping years ago. And more recently in the custom bike business.

"I'd like to come by."

"If you want a cup of coffee or you'd like to see the bike we're building, stop by anytime."

"And don't bother hitting my brakes if I'm there to talk to you about the church," Wyatt added for him.

"Sounds about right." Jeremy touched the brim of his hat and walked across the drive to his truck.

When he pulled up the drive of Back Street Church, Beth Bradshaw was sitting in front of his RV. He hadn't expected her to be the one pounding his door down trying to save this church. But why wouldn't she be the one?

Maybe, more than anyone, Beth needed to fight this battle.

He joined her on the glider bench outside his RV. She scooted to the edge, as far from him as possible.

He tried real hard not to let that hurt his ego. He figured she had a lot of reasons. One might be that she hated his guts.

That didn't sit well with him, the idea of her hating him.

He pushed the ground and the glider slid back and forth. Sitting there on the glider with her kind of felt like courting the old-fashioned way. The only thing missing was lemonade. She probably wouldn't see the humor in that, but he did. The two of them as nervous as cats sitting on a glider, what else could he think?

He had to lead the conversation in another direction, away from courting Bethlehem.

"I kind of thought you might thank me for tearing this church down, Bethlehem."

"Stop calling me that."

"It's your name."

"No one calls me Bethlehem and you know it."

He started to remind her that her mother had called her Bethlehem. Neither of them needed that memory. He glanced at the box on her lap. She had her hands around it, like a little girl holding on to a treasure.

She glanced at him, a cowgirl face with straight brown hair in twin braids and eyes that pinned him to the spot. She'd have him questioning everything about himself if she didn't stop looking at him like that.

"Why would you ever think I'd want this church torn down?" Her words were soft, matching the look in her dark eyes.

He shook his head and reined in the part of him that wanted to give her everything.

"I don't know, I guess I thought it was tied to a lot of memories that you'd want to be rid of, not memories you'd want to hang on to." He eyed that box again, wondering why in the world she'd brought it here and what it would mean to him.

Jeremy's words played through Beth's mind. She settled her gaze on the church. It was weathered and beaten down, forgotten. She'd been riding past this church her whole life, and since she'd come home from California those rides had resumed. Sometimes she even stopped and sat on the front steps.

As a teenager, when she'd felt the most alone, she'd found peace here. He wouldn't understand. He would think she was weak if she told him that she'd hidden here, trying to find answers, to find a way past the pain of losing her mom.

She cleared her throat.

"I brought you something." She reached into the box and handed him her mother's Bible. She had no idea why she wasn't keeping it for herself.

He needed it more? Maybe because she hoped something in there would stop him. He wasn't going to listen to her or anyone else.

Maybe he would listen to her mom. Her heart trembled a little, afraid of his reaction, afraid of her own reaction. He took the Bible from her hands.

"Beth, this isn't fair."

"It was my mother's."

"I can't take this."

"She would want you to have it. I think she would want you to know what she thought of you." Her hands trembled as she reached, flipping the pages of the book in his hands. "There are prayers in here, for Jason and me. Also for you and Elise."

He let out a shaky breath and she waited. He didn't react. After a few minutes he stood and walked away, still holding her mother's Bible. She considered going after him, trying to talk to him.

Her feet wouldn't move in that direction. Besides, she knew when to let a man be. This was one of those times. He walked across the church lawn, head down, the Bible in his hands. He climbed the steps and walked into the church, closing the door behind him. It didn't take a genius to know he didn't want to talk.

Guilt flooded her. For years Chance had used God's word to beat her into submission. She didn't want to do that to Jeremy. She considered going after him and apologizing.

She watched the door, waiting for him to come back out. The wind picked up. The southern sky was dark. She shivered a little and watched as clouds moved. A band of gray on the horizon meant rain and it was getting wider. Before long she'd have to hightail it for home.

A truck rumbled down the road and pulled into the crumbling parking lot that hadn't seen this much traffic in years. Jason's truck.

Her brother parked and got out. He walked toward her, his smile familiar. The one person to hold her life together, her brother. He'd always been there for her. He'd done his best to make her smile during their mother's illness and after they'd lost her. He'd been the one sending money to California as her marriage fell apart.

"What are you doing here?" He looked from the church to her and then at the darkening sky. "Did you know there's a tornado watch and a severe thunderstorm warning?"

"I heard on the news earlier that we could have storms today. It's May in Oklahoma, what's new? What are you doing here?"

He sat down next to her. "Same as you. I thought I could talk him out of it. Or maybe offer him enough money that he'd walk away."

"He doesn't need money."

"No, I guess he doesn't."

"He needs closure." She bit down on her bottom lip, letting that thought settle in. "He's a lot like dad. They both blame this church for their pain. Dad kept us away. Jeremy wants to tear the church down."

"Interesting." Jason crossed his left leg over his right knee and relaxed, as if it was just a pretty summer day and they were sharing iced tea on the front porch. Instead they were both casting cautious glances toward the southern horizon. "Where is he?"

"Inside the church."

"Hmm." Jason smiled, the way Jason did. He'd always been the one finding ways to make everyone laugh, to make them smile when they didn't feel like smiling. When he'd stopped smiling, God had sent Alyson and she'd helped him find his joy again.

He'd learned that he didn't always have to be the one lifting everyone else up. Beth loved her sister-in-law for doing that for him.

Sometimes she was jealous, that everyone seemed to be able to find someone to love them, to keep them safe. Her memories of a relationship were of abuse and fear, not safety or security. She had memories that no one would understand, so she didn't share.

"Beth, be careful."

"It's a storm, Jason. I've been through a few."

He shook his head and his smile faltered. "That isn't what I mean and I'm pretty sure you know that. Jeremy has a lot going on in his life."

"Right, and I'm not the best judge of character."

"I just don't want to see you hurt."

"I know." She smiled, for Jason. "I won't get hurt."

The wind picked up and in the distance jagged lightning flashed across the sky. Thunder rumbled and the humidity in the air was heavy. Jason pulled out his phone.

She glanced at the radar he'd pulled up on the screen. The big red blob was lingering over their area of the satellite map.

"Great." She watched the darkening clouds and trees leaning and swirling with the wind. "I guess this might be a good time to pray."

A sprinkle of rain hit her arm. Beth looked up at the sky and then at the dusty, dry ground as the raindrops hit. It had been so long since it rained that the droplets bounced and didn't soak in, not immediately.

Faith. She'd been through a drought, a long man-made drought, but faith was seeping back into her life. Her spiritual life had been a lot like hard, cracked earth, devoid of moisture. When faith started to return it was that same earth but with a trickle of water streaming through it, soaking into the dryness.

"We should probably go." Jason stood, pushing his hat back from his face as he studied the sky. "This doesn't feel right."

"What, you don't love that green sky?"

"Not particularly."

She loved the rain. She loved storms. On the drive over a DJ on the radio, probably trying to be a comedian, had played the Jo Dee Messina song, "Bring on the Rain." Beth found herself singing one line from that song, that she was not afraid.

The front door of the church opened. Jeremy stepped out on the porch. He was still carrying the Bible. Next to her, Jason made a noise and she shot him a look to silence anything he would say.

But he said it. "Is that Mom's Bible?"

"It is."

"Dad gave you the box?"

"He did."

"And you brought the Bible to Jeremy Hightree?" Jason's voice was tight, not really disapproving.

"I did. I just thought…"

"You might have pushed too far, Beth."

"Maybe. But I don't think so." She met her brother look for look. "If this doesn't work, I'm moving on to step two, and then step three."

"I knew I shouldn't have told you about the historical society." Jason murmured, then smiled and waved to Jeremy.

Jeremy Hightree walked down the steps of the church. He glanced at the sky, watched for a minute and headed in their direction. He looked relaxed, in jeans, boots and a deep red shirt. But casual was a facade on this cowboy.

Rain was misting down on them and the wind was picking up.

"Jeremy." Jason held out his hand. Jeremy took it, a quick handshake and then his gaze dropped to Beth.

She waited. And wished she was tall because then he

wouldn't have to drop his gaze to meet hers. She could face him, head on, eye to eye.

He held out the Bible. "I can't keep this."

"She cared about you."

"I know she did, but this is something she wanted you to have."

"We should go." Jason shot a quick look at the sky. "Now!"

Her brother took hold of her arm and started to pull her toward the parking lot and their trucks. Her gaze shot to the southern horizon. Wind blew against them, slowing their progress and the rain hitting Beth's face stung like ice against her skin.

A slow, loud warning siren sounded in the distance and she heard Jeremy yelling at them to stop.

Chapter Four

The tornado siren sounded as Jeremy watched Beth heading for her truck, Jason at her side. She turned to say something. Her words were lost in the strong gust of wind that hit, blowing leaves across the church lawn and small limbs from the few trees.

Jeremy scanned the horizon. A warning didn't necessarily mean a tornado on the ground. Sometimes a warning was just a warning.

This time, though, things were a little different. He could feel the energy, the hum of the storm, the vibration of it. The deafening roar echoed in the distance.

"We should head for the basement." Jeremy watched the sky as he yelled, cupping his mouth to get the sound across the wind.

Jason nodded and started back, his cell phone in his hand. Jeremy guessed he was probably calling his wife. Beth stood frozen a few feet behind Jason.

"Beth, come on."

She nodded but she didn't move. She was watching the sky, the wind blowing her hair. A gust caught her hat. She pushed it back down and held on.

Jeremy raced across the crumbling parking lot and grabbed her arm. "This is not the time to stand and watch."

The roar increased in intensity. To the south the clouds were now tumbling and rolling, a dark mass of swirling destruction.

"Hurry." He had hold of Beth's arm and she was fighting him, pulling away.

"I can make it home."

"Beth, head for the church," Jason yelled as he pushed his phone into his pocket and turned, glancing at the dark clouds and then at his sister.

Jeremy cursed under his breath and picked her up. She was light in his arms and her protests were weak. Her arms went around his neck and he didn't know if it was rain or her tears that soaked his shoulder.

"I can walk." Beth struggled a little, and he held her tight.

"I know you can but…" He shook his head, not wanting to get stuck in the storm while she watched the clouds.

As they raced to the church, pieces of insulation fell from the sky. Jeremy ducked his head into the wind. That put his face pretty close to Beth's. And she smelled so good he decided carrying her was about the best idea he'd had in a while. Or maybe the worst.

Jason was ahead of him, jerking the door of the church open. They raced through the building to the door at the back of the sanctuary. The basement was dark. The steps were narrow.

He hadn't turned on electricity to the building. There hadn't seemed to be a reason.

Jason pulled out his cell phone and lit up the steps

with a patch of blue light. Jeremy held Beth tight and followed the other man down the steps. The basement held two classrooms and a kitchen/fellowship area that had seen better days.

"The back room," Jeremy yelled, and he didn't have to. The deafening roar had been left behind. The basement was pretty quiet, and a whole lot eerie. Jason glanced back and nodded. The room in the corner was the smallest and safest.

"Let me down." Beth came back to life, fighting in his arms.

"Not until we're in that room and safe. I'm not going to let you freeze up now, or have you head back upstairs to chase tornadoes."

"I didn't freeze. I just didn't…" She shuddered in his arms. "Don't grab me again."

"I won't. Once you're safe I'll never touch you again."

Man, that wasn't a promise he wanted to keep. As much as he didn't want to admit it, she felt good in his arms.

He put her down in the corner of the room and slammed the door shut behind him. The windowless room cut them off from the rest of the world. Buried beneath the ground, it was nearly soundproof. Their cell phones glowed an unearthly blue.

He turned, surveying their shelter, flashing his cell phone around the darkness. He'd had Sunday school in this room as a kid. It had been painted white, to dispel the dark, windowless gloom. Posters of Jesus had hung on the walls to add color. There had been an easel with a felt board in the corner for paper cutouts of Jesus and the disciples.

Now the room was draped with spiderwebs that clung to his clothes. He brushed a strand from his face and hoped the resident hadn't remained behind.

Back then he'd been a kid who knew how to pray. Man, he didn't have a clue where that kid went. Somewhere along the way he'd started taking care of things on his own.

Lot of good that had done him.

He scanned the room looking for the flashlight he thought he'd left down here a few days earlier, when he'd been poking around in the old building, stirring up dust and memories. He'd left it in the kitchen.

"I have a flashlight out there." He yanked the door open and ignored objections from Jason and Beth. The flashlight was on the counter next to an old avocado-green fridge. He grabbed it and raced back to the shelter of the classroom.

Jason shook his head when Jeremy walked in, flashing the light around the room. Jason had taken a seat on the edge of an old table.

"How long do we stay down here?" Beth sat on the stool in the corner of the room, shivering, her bare arms damp from the rain that pummeled them as they ran for the church. He flashed the light in her direction and she glanced away.

Jeremy pulled off the plaid shirt he wore over his T-shirt. He tossed it to her, as if it didn't matter. But it did. When she held it in her hands and smiled it mattered a lot. She slipped her arms into the shirt and pulled it around herself.

He turned away, listening, waiting. Jason stood next to him, his cell phone up to his ear. Jason bowed his head, leaning against the wall. Jeremy put a hand on his shoulder, squeezing tight. "She's fine."

"Of course she is." Beth smiled, her words sunny and bright in the dark room. "She's Alyson and she's probably in the basement praying like crazy for everyone else."

"Someone has to pray." Jeremy looked up, listening for any signs of distress in the old church. It sounded as steady and solid as ever. He could barely hear the wind that he knew roared around them.

Or maybe the storm was done, blown over. Maybe the massive, gray funnel hadn't been a funnel. Now *that* was wishful thinking. There was only one way to find out for sure.

"I'm going up." He opened the door.

Beth choked out a sound. He turned the flashlight in her direction. Her fingers were curled around the cuffs of his shirt and she shivered.

"I don't think you should go." Her voice broke a little. Mascara streaked down her cheeks.

His hand was still on the doorknob.

"What do you suggest? Stay down here indefinitely?" He handed the flashlight over to Jason and pulled his cell phone back out of his pocket.

"Well, until we know for sure if it's over." Beth wrapped her arms around herself; his shirt swallowed her. He couldn't help but think about how her scent would linger with his on his shirt.

He needed to get his business going and leave this town as soon as possible. He was starting to doubt the wisdom in building a home here, even if it was meant only to be a weekend home, a place to escape to.

"I think it's probably over." He answered her question, smiling a little.

"It might not be."

"Beth, it's a tornado." Jason sighed and sounded more than a little frustrated. It took a lot to get Jason to that point. "They don't linger, they move on."

Jeremy nearly walked away from the door, back to Beth. He considered crossing the room and taking her in his arms until she stopped shivering.

And then he considered the fact that he might be losing his mind.

He walked out and closed the door behind him and tried not to worry about what he'd find when he got upstairs. The church could be flattened. His RV could be gone. His barn and his livestock were across the street. Who knew what had happened to them as the storm moved through.

In the basement, nothing had been disturbed. The few small windows were intact. He hurried up the stairs and opened the door to the sanctuary. The church was untouched. The air around him was still. It was silent.

It was eerie as anything.

The birds that had taken up residence in the building swooped and landed on the hanging overhead lights. He no longer needed the cell phone for light so he dialed his sister's number. She had a scanner and if her phone was working she'd be able to tell him what was going on.

The cell didn't work. He opened the front door and stepped out on the porch. His RV still stood at the edge of the parking lot. The trees were still standing. Across the road his house was no longer framed. He had to stand there for a minute, take it all in.

He took a deep breath and whistled. After a few minutes he walked off the porch and looked around. He pushed his hat back and looked up, at the building that had sheltered them during the storm. And yeah, he got the irony in that.

The church was untouched. The lawn was littered with tree limbs and debris from other people's homes, barns and businesses. Not one shingle had blown off the church roof. Not one window had been cracked.

Footsteps on the floor behind him dragged his attention back to the church and the two people who had gone through this storm with him. Jason Bradshaw was punching buttons on his phone and frowning.

"No cell service," Jeremy offered, knowing it wouldn't help Jason feel any better.

"Yeah, I have to get home and check on Alyson."

"Right. I'll make a drive through town."

Jason's steady look landed on his sister. Beth stood at the edge of the porch. She still wore Jeremy's shirt.

"Are you staying here or going with Jason?" Jeremy stood at the bottom of the steps looking up at her. Somehow he'd managed to sound casual. That wasn't easy when she was standing there with his shirt swallowing her petite frame. Once, a long time ago, she'd worn his jacket on a cool night. He remembered her scent had lingered on it, floral and citrus. That took him back to places he didn't want to go. Or maybe he did. That was the problem.

"I'll go with you." She walked down the steps and stood next to Jeremy.

Jason shook his head as he shoved the useless phone back in his pocket. "Obviously the phone towers have been hit. There could be power lines down across the roads."

"Jason, we'll be careful." Beth smiled at her brother.

Jeremy wasn't part of a "we." He'd never been part of a "we." He'd have to explain that to her. He'd managed to live a whole life on his own. But now wasn't the time for that discussion.

Instead he found himself as part of a "we."

"We've been through a few of these storms, Jason." Jeremy winked at Beth. "We'll be careful."

Jason's ever-present smile faded. "She's my sister."

"Right, I get that. I'm going to try and make it to the nursing home to check on my mom. I also want to make sure this didn't hit Grove."

Beth smiled at him, and then a softer smile for her overprotective brother. "Jason, go check on Alyson. We'll be safe."

Jason rubbed a hand across his forehead and grinned a little easier. "Yeah, okay, I'm cutting the apron strings, sis."

"Good, they were getting a little tight." She took a few steps and stopped in front of her brother. Rising to her tiptoes she kissed his cheek. "You're the best."

"Yeah, I like to think so. I'll be back soon or meet up with the two of you later." Jason walked across the lawn toward his truck. He stopped once and leaned to pick up an envelope in the lawn.

Typical of a storm, debris from other locations landed miles from home. Jeremy let out a sigh and surveyed the landscape that two hours earlier had been whole.

The church hadn't been touched. Beth smiled and started to point that out to Jeremy. Instead she let it go.

No use stating the obvious. And Jeremy had walked away. He was studying the debris in the yard.

Beth turned her attention to the property across the street. The frame of his house was gone. The barn was missing a piece of sheet metal from the roof. She shook her head and walked back to Jeremy's side.

"I'm sorry about your house."

He shrugged and smiled. "It missed the church."

"It would have saved you a lot of time if it hadn't."

"Yeah, I guess it would have saved some explaining, too. People would be a lot more forgiving if it got torn down during an act of God, and not by me."

"Maybe God is trying to tell you something." Beth had meant to tease, but it hadn't come out that way.

"I doubt that, Beth. The church has to go. I have plans for a building. I have a guy already selling his house to move here and manage things."

"I think you should have an alternate plan."

"What does that mean?" He stood in front of her, tall, his eyes pinning her down.

"I'm still going to stop you."

He grinned, slow and easy and she had a moment of serious doubt. "You're pretty sure of that, aren't you?"

She matched him with a smile of her own. "I'm very sure."

"Let the games begin. Because as much as you don't want that church torn down, honey, I do."

Sirens in the distance ended the dance. Jeremy walked to the edge of the church parking lot and she followed. Beth stopped next to him and closed her eyes. She let the soft words of a prayer fill her mind, a prayer for her community, for the injured if there were any, for homes and businesses lost. For strength. It had been more years than she could count since the area was hit by a tornado.

She opened her eyes and looked up at Jeremy. He gave her an easy smile. Her heart did the two-step, obviously forgetting that they were on opposing sides.

A police car pulled into the church parking lot, a county deputy that she didn't know. They'd probably called in reserve officers to handle the situation. The car stopped behind Jeremy's truck.

"Checking to make sure everyone is okay." The officer got out of his car. It was the normal routine after a storm like this, to go through the area making sure people weren't trapped or injured. Or worse.

"We're fine." Jeremy slid his fingers through hers and they walked across the debris-strewn lawn toward the officer.

"How bad is it?" Beth asked, wanting to know but a little afraid to hear the answer.

"Pretty bad. Estimates are that it stayed on the ground for about twenty miles. There's a small area of Dawson that was hit pretty good. It leveled a few homes, more are damaged and Dawson Community Church lost part of its roof. The school sustained some damage so we're going to have to find somewhere to set up a shelter."

"What about the nursing home? Was it damaged?" Jeremy held tight to her hand and she gave his a little squeeze. His mom had never been there for her kids, but she was still his mom.

"Nursing home is fine. They have a backup generator and no damage."

"And Grove?" Jeremy's sister lived in Grove.

"Grove didn't even get a thunderstorm and the cell is breaking up now."

"Where will people go?" Beth couldn't imagine her town without the Community Church, or with friends moving because houses had been destroyed.

"Not sure yet. With the school and the Community Church out of commission we're pretty limited on suitable shelters." The officer got back into his car. "Folks might have to go to Grove or even to Tulsa if they don't have family to stay with."

"What about here?" She didn't look at Jeremy. "I'm sorry, it isn't mine to offer, but the church is intact. There's plenty of room."

"Beth." Jeremy's voice was soft, raspy.

She forced herself to meet his eyes. She wouldn't be afraid. Nope, she'd just plow through and suffer the consequences. Jeremy's jaw clenched and he glanced away, back at the church.

"Sir?" The officer was in his car, window down and the engine idling quietly.

Jeremy looked at Beth and then he shook his head and smiled. "They can use the church as a shelter."

The officer nodded and then the patrol car backed away, turning and pulling out of the drive. It cruised down Back Street toward town, lights flashing but no siren.

Jeremy looked down at her, shaking his head. Beth waited, because he still had hold of her hand. Her mind flashed back a few years, to Chance, to the times when she'd pushed him too far. "Beth?"

She shook her head. "I'm sorry. It wasn't my place to offer the church."

"No, it wasn't. You win this round, but we're not finished." He reached for her hand. "And stop looking so worried. As mad as you make me, I'd never hurt you."

He leaned close, pulling off his hat and raising her hand to hold it close to his chest, close to the steady rhythm of his heart. His gaze locked with hers. "I've never hit a woman and I don't plan on starting now. Even if you drive me crazy. I won't hurt you."

"I…" What did she say to that?

Before she could think of anything to say, he moved closer.

He touched her cheek and then his lips settled on the scar above her eye. And she didn't pull away. As his kiss trailed down to her cheek she fought a shred of panic. She fought the confusing urge to fall into his arms. She fought tears that burned her eyes because for a long time she'd felt like pieces of a woman and she longed to be whole.

Jeremy stepped away from her, and she could breathe again. She could think.

"We should drive into town and see what needs to be done. And I'd like to find a way to check on my mom." He sounded as if he was looking for a way out of this moment, too. As if he too needed space to breathe.

Beth nodded because for the moment she couldn't gather words to respond.

She looked back at the church as he opened the passenger door of his truck for her to get in. The church had a reprieve. But for how long?

"The church is safe, Beth. It's still standing and tonight if people need a place to stay, it'll be here."

"I know." She climbed into his truck and he closed the door.

Back Street intersected with Main Street. Main Street ran north and south. Tulsa was over an hour away.

Dawson Crossing, the town had been named back in the 1800s. Folks had shortened it to Dawson and it sometimes got confused with a larger community close to Tulsa.

Today Dawson looked as if someone other than Jeremy had been turned loose with a dozer. On the outskirts of town several homes were demolished. Nothing remained of those homes but foundations with scattered, splintered lumber. Home after home had been damaged. Trees were down, power lines hung from broken poles and roofs were partially gone. In town the convenience store had lost the roof over the gas pumps and the windows were shattered.

The Mad Cow Café didn't look too worse for wear. There were shingles missing, but other than that, Vera looked happy to still have her business. She stood out front, her apron tight around her waist. When she saw Beth and Jeremy, she waved. Jeremy stopped his truck and backed up.

"Is the café okay, Vera?" Jeremy leaned forward and Beth leaned back in the seat, giving him a clear view of the Mad Cow's proprietor.

"It sure is. I have a generator on the way so hopefully I won't lose all my groceries. But I'm one of the lucky ones."

"Is there anything we can do?" Beth asked.

"Not yet, Beth. I did hear that Jeremy's going to open the church as a shelter. Do you need blankets?"

Jeremy blinked a few times at how quickly word traveled in this town. He was all for letting people stay in the church. The word shelter implied a lot more than he had really planned.

"I haven't thought about it, Vera. I just planned on

leaving the door open for anyone who needs a place to stay."

"Bless your heart." Vera stepped off the sidewalk. Her dark hair was shot through with gray and her skirt and blouse were not as crisp as usual. She walked up to the truck and leaned in the window. "Honey, you need to move the pews and make room for cots. Wyatt Johnson has quite a few in storage at the Community Church. They also have blankets and other emergency supplies. The Red Cross will be showing up, too."

Go Wyatt. Jeremy just smiled.

Beth jumped into the conversation. "We'll need flashlights and plenty of bottled water."

Vera patted her arm. "Already taken care of. Jason was through here earlier and he's going to bring a tank of water and set it up at the church."

Jeremy accepted that the church wouldn't turn itself into a shelter. But people in Dawson were prepared the way they were always prepared. People here knew that in the space of a heartbeat, life brought change. He'd experienced plenty of change in his own life.

In the last few weeks he'd gone from being a guy with a plan to the guy everyone wanted to stop. And now this. He shook his head and he let it go because his plans being halted were nothing compared to people losing their homes.

"I guess we should get on the road and see if there's anything else we can do." Jeremy shifted into gear. "See you later, Vera."

"Okay, but be careful. And don't worry, I'll bring up a big batch of barbecued pork for sandwiches to feed anyone that shows up this evening."

"Thanks, Vera." Beth reached through the window and gave Vera's hand a squeeze.

"Do you mind riding along with me while I check on my mom?" He shifted his truck into gear and peered to the left, at a field littered with debris, including what looked like it might have been part of someone's roof.

"Of course not."

He slowed as they neared emergency vehicles, lights flashing. A first responder in an oversize coat stepped out to stop them and then walked up to his window. Jeremy waited.

"Got power lines down in the road, Jeremy. I can't let you drive through." The volunteer was young, maybe in his late teens. Jeremy wasn't sure if he should know the kid or not. But the kid knew his name so he guessed he must.

"I need to get to the nursing home to check on my mom."

"Yeah, there isn't a way to get there right now. Part of the Lawtons' barn is in the road up here, and farther up there's a big old tree across the road."

"Thanks, I'll try again this evening."

The volunteer in his gray jacket with neon stripes nodded. His safety helmet was loose, a little large on his head. The jacket swam around his thin frame. But in a small community, it took everyone to pitch in when disaster struck.

Jeremy backed his truck into a drive that led to someone's field. He pulled around and headed back to Dawson. Beth leaned back in her seat and sighed. He glanced her way.

"I can drive you back to your place," he offered, slowing as the truck got close to a side road that would lead them to the Bradshaw ranch.

"I'm not in any hurry."

Yeah, neither was he. Even at thirty, he didn't want to meet up with Buck Bradshaw. Beth's dad was a big man and probably still willing to take care of business if anyone messed with his little girl.

"Remember your sixteenth birthday?"

She turned pink, so he knew she remembered.

"I remember."

He'd kissed Beth on her sixteenth birthday. They'd been at a rodeo and her friends had teased her for smiling at him. Later he'd led her to the creek and held her close, enjoying the feel of her in his arms. He hadn't been quite eighteen. She'd been so far out of his reach, it had been like grasping at a star.

And her dad had caught them down there. Man, he'd cussed Jeremy a blue streak.

"Jeremy, watch out." Beth's scream coincided with Jeremy hitting the brakes as a woman rushed into the road right in front of them.

The woman waved her arms, panic etched into a pale face. A trickle of blood on her cheek smeared when she brushed her hand across her face.

"What in the world?" Beth was unbuckling her seat belt. "That's Keira Hanson."

"Hang tight, Beth." Jeremy pulled to the side of the road. The woman ran to the passenger side of the truck, stumbling through the grassy ditch to get to them. She was trembling and the blood oozed from a cut on the side of her face.

"Keira, what's wrong?" Beth already had her door open. "Get in and we'll drive you up to your place."

"It's Mark. He was in the barn when this hit and part of the building collapsed." She sobbed, leaning into the truck. "I couldn't call for help and I couldn't get him out on my own."

"Beth, I'm going to run on up there. You take my truck and drive back to that roadblock. Tell them to get help up here."

Jeremy unbuckled his seat belt and set the emergency brake. Beth was already scooting over and he opened the door and stepped out of the truck as she slid behind the wheel. He watched as she adjusted the seat and shifted into gear.

"Be careful." Her voice was soft and her eyes tore him up. And he thought maybe no one else had ever cared about him as much as Beth and her mamma.

He watched as she turned his truck back in the direction they'd come from and then he started up the long dirt and gravel drive.

He didn't know what he'd find when he reached the Hansons' barn, but he prayed that Mark would be alive. It had been a long time since he'd prayed. And he was thankful that God had a good memory.

"Jeremy will find him, Keira." Beth shifted and hit the gas to speed down the paved road. "He'll be just fine."

"I keep praying that's true, Beth. But what if…"

Keira pushed her hands against her eyes and Beth shot a quick look around the cab for something Keira could hold against the cut on her face. She slowed down and reached for the glove box. It opened to reveal napkins from fast food restaurants.

"Keira, grab those and hold them against the cut to stop the bleeding."

Keira nodded and reached into the glove box.

"What if he's…" Keira sobbed and neither of them needed for her to finish that sentence.

"He isn't." Relief flooded Beth when the flashing lights of first responders came into view. She pulled up to Kenny Gordon, the kid who had been directing traffic minutes earlier.

"Beth, the road's still closed." The kid grinned.

"I know, Kenny. Listen, we need help up at Keira's place. The barn collapsed and Mark is inside."

Kenny got serious. He lifted his two-way and told someone on the other end that they needed a team to head up to the Hanson place. He finished the call and leaned in the window.

"They'll be up there in five minutes, Keira. We'll find him, don't you worry."

Keira nodded and a fresh batch of tears streamed down her face, mixing with dirt and blood.

"Kenny, do you have a first aid kit?"

The kid nodded. "Got one in the truck over there. Hang tight a sec and I'll get it for you."

Beth reached for Keira's hand. "Keira, we'll find him."

"I'm really trying to pray, Beth. The only thing I can get out is, 'God, don't let him die.'"

"I think that's a prayer." Beth had been saying plenty of her own prayers since all of this started. She didn't think God was expecting long prayers, not at a time like this.

Kenny was back with the first aid kit. He had already taken out a few wipes, salve and a Band-Aid. Beth tore the top off the antiseptic wipe and pulled it out for Keira.

"Clean the wound and then we'll put this on it."

Keira nodded. She gasped when the wipe hit the cut, but she cleaned it and the side of her face before taking the Band-Aid from Beth.

"Thanks, Kenny."

"Maybe you all should stick around here until the responders can get up there and clear things up a little." Kenny's gaze shot past Beth to Keira and Beth knew what he meant. She wondered if that was his idea or the idea of one of his supervisors, someone who didn't want Keira on hand when they found her husband.

"We have to go back." Keira's voice was shaky. "Kenny, thank you for thinking of me, but I have to be there."

Kenny handed Beth the first aid kit. "In case you need it."

Beth backed the truck up the same way Jeremy had earlier. She turned and headed back in the direction of the Hanson farm.

And she prayed, because God wasn't the dictator that Chance had wanted her to believe. God hadn't forced her to stay in a marriage that kept her prisoner to a man who beat her and locked her in the bathroom when she talked about leaving.

God hadn't wanted that for her. And now she was free. She was free and she knew that God heard her prayers.

Sirens behind her warned that the emergency crews were on the way. She pulled to the side of the road and allowed the big yellow truck and first responder rescue unit to pass. She followed them up the long, rutted driveway that led to the Hansons' place.

When they pulled up to the barn, Keira jumped out of the truck. One of the first responders stopped her. She fought against him, wanting to get close to the barn.

Beth hurried to her side. "Keira, let them find him. If we stay back, they'll be able to work more quickly."

Keira slumped against Beth's side. "I can't do this. I can't stand here and I can't breathe."

"Sit down." Beth eased the woman to the ground. "Slow down, breathe easy so you don't pass out. When they find Mark, he needs to see you here, waiting for him. He's going to need for you to be calm."

Keira nodded but she was still gasping, still sobbing. And Beth wasn't going to tell her she shouldn't be upset. She would be frantic if it was someone she loved in that barn.

She scanned the area, looking for Jeremy. She spotted him, pulling boards off the building. He'd pulled on leather work gloves and he ripped at metal from the caved-in roof. He turned, as if he knew she was watching. His smile was weary, his T-shirt soaked with perspiration. She curled her fingers around the cuffs of the shirt he'd given her.

He pulled off more boards and then went down on all fours and crawled into the hole he'd made. Beth wrapped her arms around a sobbing Keira and held her close.

"They'll find him," Beth whispered, to herself and to assure Keira.

Seconds ticked by and then minutes. Beth glanced at her watch. The tornado had hit more than two hours earlier. She tried not to think about how seriously injured Mark might be and what that amount of time meant to him. She closed her eyes and prayed they'd find him soon.

Boards and metal scraps were being tossed aside. Men worked with crowbars and anything else they could find to move the rubble of the barn. Neighbors had shown up to help.

"Here he is." Jeremy shouted the alarm from somewhere under the pile of lumber.

Keira jumped up, wobbling. Beth held on to her arm.

"Keira, we have to stay back."

They watched as several men ran to join Jeremy, who had backed out of the tunnel he'd made in the rubble of the barn. An ambulance pulled closer. Its blue lights flashed. The crew moved silently, pulling medical equipment and a stretcher from the back of the vehicle.

The first responders continued to remove the rubble that covered the area where Jeremy had found Mark Hanson.

"He's going to be fine." Beth held on to Keira, who was a few years older than herself. Life hadn't been easy for the Hansons. Keira had suffered three miscarriages in the last few years. Mark had lost his job.

Beth swallowed, pushed aside doubt. And then there was a shout. They had Mark. They were talking to him. And then they were easing him out of the mangled pile of wood and metal that used to be their barn. As he lay on the ground, he turned, looking for his wife.

Keira tore loose from Beth's arms and ran to her husband. They hugged and Keira kissed his face, kissed his head. The paramedics stabilized his leg while Keira held his hand. And Beth wanted to laugh and cry, all at once. Salty tears trickled down her cheeks and she wiped them away with the back of her hand.

Faith. A couple that held on to each other.

Beth searched the crowd for Jeremy.

Jeremy pulled off his gloves and walked toward Beth. He smiled at the tear-stained face and wavering smile that greeted him.

"Looks like he has a broken leg, but he'll be fine."

Beth sniffled. "Yeah, but how can they take one more blow? They've lost babies, lost his job. What if they lose this farm, too?"

"It looks to me like they'll be happy to have each other."

"I get that, but seriously, how many times can a couple get knocked down?"

Boy, she was going for the jugular. "I don't know, Beth."

"No, you don't. I'm sorry."

"Look, I know you're upset about the church. But I can give Mark Hanson a job when I get the shop built. Once he's recovered, I can put him to work."

She looked up at him, her brown eyes huge and tears spilling out again, running down her cheeks. "You're cut and you're limping."

"I got tangled in some sheet metal when I was digging through that mess. And the limp is old news and nothing a few aspirin won't fix."

Beth reached for his hand and led him back to his truck. He thought about pulling away from her, but he didn't listen to his good sense very often. This time he completely kicked it to the curb.

If good sense meant cutting loose from Beth Bradshaw, he didn't need it right now. There'd be time for regret later.

She opened the door of his truck and pulled out a first aid kit. While he stood there like an idiot, she wiped his cuts. Her fingers were gentle, touching his arm and then his cheek. She pulled out a butterfly bandage for his arm, the deeper of the two cuts.

"It's just a scratch on your face, but the cut on your arm might need stitches."

"I'm sure it's fine." He swallowed as she settled the adhesive strip in place.

"There, all done."

"Thank you."

Her hand was still on his arm, her touch sweeter than honey. She sniffled and stared up at him. "You'd really give him a job?"

"Beth, I know this might be news to you, but I'm not the enemy." He let out a heavy sigh. "I'm not the enemy."

He brushed his fingers across her cheek and wiped away the tears that had spilled out again.

"I know you're not. But the church…"

He rubbed his hand across his face and waited. He could walk away. He could tell her he didn't want to discuss this with her. But those big brown eyes were looking up, intent, searching. She was all kinds of trouble he hadn't expected.

"I know it doesn't make sense, Beth. But I'm a long way from being that poor kid that went to Back Street. Then again, I'm not. I'm still the kid who stole vegetables from neighbors' gardens, and worked until bedtime to buy what we needed."

The words kind of surprised him because he'd never

said them aloud to anyone. She had stripped away his control with soft questions and tear-filled eyes.

Jeremy reached into the truck for his hat and pushed it down on his head, calling himself a few choice names. Beth was standing in front of him, teary-eyed and tired. She didn't need an info dump.

"Beth, I'm sorry."

She shook her head. "No, I am. It was my fault for pushing you."

"No, it wasn't. You said what everyone else has been thinking and maybe you're right. But I guess that doesn't mean I'm going to change my mind."

"I know and I do understand." And then she smiled, bright as summer sunshine after a storm. A storm like the one they'd just been through. "But I am going to stop you."

"I don't know how. It's my land and I'm all set. I just have to get the final permit from planning and zoning."

Her brows shot up and her expression changed, making him wonder. He had a bad feeling. No one knew small-town politics better than he did. He'd been dealing with the city of Dawson for weeks, trying to get things squared away so he could move forward.

"We should go." Right, they should go. And he figured he should plan on a battle for the church.

"I can drive you to your house now, if you want."

"My truck is at the church."

"Gotcha."

The ambulance was pulling away. As it headed down the drive, a few trucks pulled up. Jeremy knew it was time to hit the road as Tim Cooper and several of his sons got out of one of their big Ford F-350s.

"Let's hit the road." Jeremy walked around to the tailgate of his truck. He'd left tools out that he needed to store in the box before they left.

Before he could get them all in the toolbox, someone called his name. He turned as Reese Cooper headed in his direction. Tim Cooper stood next to the truck Reese had gotten out of. Jeremy nodded at the other man. They shared DNA, that was it.

The day after Jeremy's mother interrupted services at Back Street Church to tell the world who her son's father was, Tim Cooper had offered Jeremy a big check. Not an apology, just a check. Jeremy had ripped the paper into pieces and walked away. He'd made the grand announcement that he'd do just fine on his own. He'd gotten a scholarship to ride on a college rodeo team. He'd already made some money riding bulls. He didn't need anything the Coopers had.

He skipped another glance in the direction of Tim Cooper before he switched back and focused on Reese. At one time he had needed family. By the time he turned eighteen that need had been left in the dust.

Reese stopped in front of him. Younger by just a couple of years, Reese was one of the more serious members of the Cooper clan. He didn't have Jackson's attitude or ladies'-man personality. He wasn't a clown like Travis. He wasn't full of himself like Blake. He wasn't nearly as likable, in Jeremy's opinion, as Jesse.

"How's Mark?" Reese rocked back on his heels a little.

"Broken leg."

Reese nodded. He shot a nervous glance in the direction of his father and then landed his direct gaze back on Jeremy. "Need some help getting a shelter set up at Back Street?"

Jeremy shrugged. "I don't have a clue, Reese. I'm not sure who all will be there or what needs to be done. I'm heading that way now to see where to start."

"We'll be over to help." It was a statement, not a question. The younger man didn't leave room for objections. Jeremy smiled a little easier. Reese Cooper was his half brother. He respected him for cowboying up and not backing down.

"That's fine, Reese." Jeremy shot a look past Reese, in the direction of Tim and a couple of his sons. "Tell your dad he can stay home."

Reese opened his mouth and closed it pretty quickly. "Sure, I'll tell him. Hey, I joined the army. I'm going to basic next week."

Respect. Jeremy slapped Reese on the back. "That's amazing."

"Yeah, well, a friend of mine from Tulsa went over a few years ago. He didn't make it back."

"You'll make it back, Reese." Beth stepped into the conversation. She hugged Reese tight. "We'll have a big party when you come home."

"I'm counting on that, Beth." Reese stepped back from the two of them. He tipped his hat in farewell and walked back to the Coopers.

"Girls." Jeremy twirled his fingers in the end of Beth's brown hair, letting the silken strands slip through his hand. He wanted to bury his fingers in the dark strands and taste the gloss she'd pulled from her pocket and swiped across her lips just moments earlier.

She wrinkled her nose at him, the way she'd done

way back when. It should have undone thoughts of kissing her, it didn't.

"Girls?" She smiled and her left brow arched a little higher than the right. "What does that mean?"

"Yeah, girls. You're sappy and sweet, and you smell good." He leaned in a little, proving to himself that his words were right on the mark.

She was wearing his shirt and she smelled like some flowery shampoo, making this feel a lot more complicated than he'd expected.

"That isn't what you used to say." She whispered the words so softly it snagged his heart.

"Yeah, I was a dumb kid who thought girls were gross."

"I remember."

She walked away, glancing back over her shoulder. He laughed a little and followed her to the truck. She already had her door open and was climbing in when he got there.

"Beth, someday I hope you'll forgive me."

She cocked her head to one side as she buckled the seat belt. "Jeremy, I hope you'll forgive yourself and a lot of other people."

He closed the door and as he walked around to his side, he glanced across the lawn to the group of Coopers who were busy cleaning up the debris-strewn lawn. Yeah, he had people to forgive.

The driveway up to the Bradshaw ranch was lined with trees, all of which were still standing. Jeremy turned and headed up the long blacktop lane toward the big brick house where Beth had grown up. Halfway to the church Beth had asked to stop and check on her family.

"You can relax," she said, dimples in her cheeks punctuating a smile that hit him in the midsection. Sweeter than a speckled pup; he'd once heard an old-timer use that expression about his wife when he'd met her.

"Relax?" He rolled his shoulders and tried to pretend he didn't have a clue what she meant by that.

"You're all tense. Do you think my dad is going to jerk you out of the truck and tell you to stay away from his little girl?"

He glanced her way and winked. "The thought did cross my mind."

He was a dozen years beyond that scraggly kid with the holey jeans and the second-hand boots.

"He'll be too distracted to think about it." She smiled and rolled down the truck window. "He's dating some-one, I think."

"I guess that's good." He slowed to a stop in front of the house. "Here we are."

He was acting like a kid on his first date. They both knew where they were, and this was anything but a date. The knots in his gut weren't about Beth Bradshaw. That twisted-up feeling was about the turn of events that had put his plans on hold.

Back Street Church had been spared. No way was he going to think that it had anything to do with Beth, the prayers of Dawson's well-meaning citizens, or anything God wanted from him.

Beth didn't move real fast to get out of the truck. Her dad was standing in front of the barn with Jason and

Alyson. Buck Bradshaw glanced in their direction, his mouth settling in a firm line. Jason said something and their father shook his head.

"I thought you said there wasn't anything to worry about?"

Next to her, Jeremy's tone teased as he asked the question. She smiled and opened the door. "There isn't."

She was out of the truck and heading toward her dad when Jeremy caught up with her. She glanced sideways. He was tall and all lean muscle. He walked with the slightest limp that she only noticed when he moved faster than his normal casual swagger. He'd broken his leg a few years ago. She remembered hearing folks in the Mad Cow talking about it for weeks. A bad break that had nearly ended his career.

"Have you been to town?" Jason asked as they approached. His hand was on his wife's waist. Alyson was four months pregnant; the baby bump barely showed beneath her shirt.

Jeremy pushed his hat back. Beth watched him glance from her dad and back to Jason. She settled her focus on her dad.

"The road to the nursing home is blocked, but they said it didn't suffer any damage. I guess you know about the houses on the west side of town?" Jeremy reached to pet the collie that had strayed onto their place a few months ago.

"I heard that you're going to open the church up for a shelter." Jason shifted his attention to Beth. "That's going to help a lot."

"Yeah, I guess it will. If you all start calling this an answer to prayer, I'll…"

Beth smiled at him, "What, take it back?"

"Yeah, maybe."

Alyson cleared her throat. "I have piles of extra blankets and I'll box up snacks and cereal."

That's when Beth's dad spoke up, his voice raspy and a little gruff. "I've got extra cots in the barn and a small generator that I can bring over."

Beth shot Jason a surprised look, because their dad had steered clear of all things Back Street for a very long time.

Beth's heart squeezed a little as she watched her dad come to grips with something inside himself. Eighteen years was a long time to hold on to anger. It had aged him beyond his sixty years.

"The cots and blankets will help, I'm sure." Jeremy pulled off his hat and ran a hand through short, brown hair. "I really don't have a clue what they're going to need. I'm letting them use the building, that's about all I know. And I guess I'd better head that way to see what I need to do."

"I should go with you to get my truck. And I can help get things set up," Beth added.

"I'll take you in a bit. We have a few things to do around here." Her dad's words stopped Beth's departure.

She could go with Jeremy. Or she could let her dad protect her. She understood, so this time she smiled a goodbye to Jeremy who nodded and walked away.

Chapter Five

Jeremy drove back to the church alone. But man, it still felt as if Beth was in his truck. Her perfume had taken up residence in the fabric, in his mind. He rolled down the windows and let fresh air blow through the cab of his truck, trying to rid himself of her presence.

The tornado didn't seem possible, not now with the blue sky and the sun streaming down. It looked like a perfect spring day. But blue skies or not, Dawson had been hit hard. The flattened outbuildings, the damaged homes, the flashing lights of emergency vehicles scouring the area, it was all part of the sickening reality.

The parking lot of Back Street Church was no longer empty. There were a couple of cars, a church van from the Community Church and a pickup truck with the Cooper Ranch logo on the doors.

And there was a big yellow bulldozer. He'd forgotten he'd arranged to have it delivered this week. Talk about bad timing. Jeremy pulled up next to the thirty-foot RV he'd been living in and parked.

His gaze settled back on the Coopers' truck parked a short distance away. He'd avoided the Coopers like the plague since he'd gotten back to town and today they were crashing into his life from all sides.

He pocketed his keys and stepped out of his rig. There were people on the wide front porch of the church. Jeremy headed that way, not real thrilled that his space had been invaded. His plans had been changed. A quick glance up at the sky and he really had to wonder what God was thinking.

One of the men on the church porch turned toward him. The cowboy hat slanted low over the man's eyes didn't hide his identity. Jackson Cooper. He wore his ranch money like old jeans. He was comfortable with his life, with his family. Jackson was the Cooper most likely to speak his mind, most likely to fight for a friend and the most likely to get knocked in the head on any given day.

Travis stood behind him. Lean and a little cagey, Travis had been adopted from somewhere in Eastern Europe when he was about five. Jeremy remembered the little kid in church, jabbering in Russian. Everyone liked Travis, when he wasn't getting on their nerves.

"What are you two doing here?" Jeremy walked up the steps, a little slower than earlier. A sharp pain in his left leg reminded him of pins and metal that kept things together these days.

"Here to help, bro." Travis grinned and tossed Jeremy a bottle of water. "We came bearing gifts."

"I'm not your bro." Jeremy set the water on the floor of the porch.

Jackson shot Travis a look and the younger brother sauntered off. Jackson stepped forward, acting as if he was going to play older brother to Jeremy, as well. That would be the day. Jackson took off his hat, swiped a hand through shaggy hair then grinned.

"Do you need me to knock that chip off your shoulder?" Jackson was no longer smiling.

"I don't think you could." Jeremy picked up the water bottle. "I need to see what's going on in there."

"They're moving pews and setting up cots. Wyatt and Ryder brought supplies."

"Good, we can have a revival later."

Jackson laughed, "Yeah, I'm with you on that. We'll let them play church. But helping neighbors isn't just for the church crowd. Helping family isn't, either."

"We're not family." This was getting real old. Jeremy shot Jackson a look that he hoped conveyed that sentiment.

"Jeremy, let me tell you something." Jackson stepped closer. "I might not agree with everything my family does. I don't join them on Sundays for church. But I can tell you this, the Cooper family sticks together. *All* of us."

Time for a reminder. "Jackson, no one would even know I was a part of the Cooper family if my mom hadn't gotten drunk and showed up at church to announce to the world that Tim Cooper owed her."

A grin split Jackson's too-handsome mug. "Yeah, that was about the best day in church I've ever had."

"Yeah, I can imagine that it was exciting for everyone."

"You and I both know that Dad should have come to you sooner. It was a big conversation between my folks, that Dad should have done something."

"Your mom is a forgiving woman."

"Yeah, she is that." Jackson shoved his hat back on his head. "She's always asking about you."

"Tell her I'm doing fine. You can tell Tim the same."

"Right, you've made a lot of money and you can buy your revenge." Jackson nodded in the direction of the dozer. "So, you plan on taking out the plaque up front that dedicates the church to the people in the community? You know, our great-grandfather donated this land. Funny that you own it now and you're going to tear down what he helped build."

Jeremy hadn't known that, and he didn't really want to hear it right now. He let the anger roll off his back. He wasn't going to punch Jackson Cooper, not right here on the steps of the Back Street Church. He also wasn't going to let him get under his skin.

"Since you probably haven't darkened the door of any church for years, don't think you can give me a Sunday school lesson on forgiveness."

"Right, I guess I can't. I guess we both have to get past this. But for right now, there are people needing help. Our help. That's what the Coopers do, we help our community."

"Last time I checked, I'm a Hightree."

Jackson leaned in close. "You're a Cooper. You look in a mirror, buddy, and you tell me you aren't a Cooper."

"Do you guys think you can give it a rest and help us set up cots?" Wyatt Johnson stood in the door of the church. "Later we'll get out the boxing gloves and the two of you can fight it out."

"I don't need gloves." Jackson slapped Jeremy on the back.

"Right, me neither." He shrugged it off. "What do we need to do?"

Wyatt motioned them into the church. Shop lights had been placed around the room, hooked from electric cords to an extension cord to the generator that hummed outside the building. The lights were bright inside a building that hadn't seen electricity in a few years.

For the first time Jeremy looked around at families he had grown up with. In the corner of the church a young mom sat with her little girl on her lap. A boy played at her feet. The mom glanced up at him, her eyes wide in a pale face.

They'd lost their home. He shoved off his anger with the Coopers and called himself a few choice names. Community mattered. He should know that. Man, he'd been on the receiving end of this town's charity more times than he could count. As a kid he'd had shoes and he and his sister had warm coats because of this church and the people in this town.

He'd been able to rodeo because Wyatt and Ryder Johnson hadn't minded loaning him a horse. Clint Cameron had taught him to ride bulls.

Tim Cooper had offered to pay him off when the news broke that Tim was his dad. By that time, Jeremy had been too angry to take a dime from the Coopers. He'd let Tim put money in the bank for Jane, because she deserved something. She'd blown through the money in no time flat.

The woman in the corner of the church looked away from him, because he'd been staring. He started to turn but the plaque Jackson had mentioned caught his attention. How he'd missed it before, he didn't know. It was wood and brass, but too far away for him to read.

The plaque was a reminder of more than the history of this church. It meant he had a whole set of ancestors he hadn't thought about, and more ties to this church than he'd ever dreamed of. Because he was a Cooper, no matter what his last name.

He pulled himself back to the moment at hand and turned to find Wyatt Johnson.

"What about food? Do you have everything you need?"

"Vera brought soup and sandwiches," Wyatt replied. "We need clothes for these kids, though."

"I can help you there." Jeremy glanced around, at the kids, their parents. "If you get sizes I'll make a trip to Grove and get whatever you need. Or I can get gift cards that we can hand out so they can get what they need."

Wyatt nodded, his smile tight. "That will be good."

A car honked as they were setting up a few more cots. More people had arrived. Families milled in the yard, looking lost, looking empty. Kids sat quietly on the porch playing with a few scattered toys.

The empty, forgotten Back Street Church had suddenly been remembered. Ironic, Jeremy decided. They needed it again and suddenly it was an important part of the town.

The car horn honked again. He walked outside to see what was going on. Jason Bradshaw's truck pulled into a parking space. Jason jumped out, leaving the engine idling and the lights on. Through the windshield Jeremy could see Beth in the passenger seat. Jason hurried across the lawn. Jeremy walked down the steps to meet him. Jason was frowning, which wasn't a good sign.

"What's up?" Wyatt must have seen Jason, too. He walked across the yard, bypassing Jeremy.

"The McCormicks can't find Darla."

"Who's Darla?" Jeremy figured he was probably the only one who didn't know. Jackson had left the church and joined them in the yard. Travis was coming down the stairs.

Boy, when something happened in Dawson, it really was a situation of calling in the cavalry. The good ole Western kind of cavalry. The kind that brought cowboys in worn boots and familiar smiles, and concern in eyes that usually teased.

"What's up?" Jackson quickly shed his normal "who cares" attitude.

"Darla McCormick was walking home from a friend's house this afternoon when the storm hit. Her parents can't find her."

"Where do we start looking?" Jeremy looked to Wyatt, because it seemed to be his call.

"We can each take a section of land," Wyatt said. "On foot, not horseback. We need to check every inch of pasture and even the roadside."

For miles, Jeremy thought. He'd picked up mail from areas that were miles away. That's what a tornado did. Man, if he had a kid, he'd be going crazy by now. He'd be racing through the countryside like a madman. Where were Darla's parents?

"Where's her family?" He'd gone to school with Mark McCormick.

"They're with their pastor. She's just ten," Jason answered.

"We need to pray now and then join the search." Wyatt took off his hat. Jeremy looked at Jackson. The two of them took off their hats and Jeremy held his against his heart. He'd prayed for friends when they'd taken a hard hit on a bull. It wasn't like he didn't believe. He'd just had a real dry spell when it came to faith.

But he knew that prayers got answered.

A kid was lost somewhere and she could definitely use some of those answered prayers. He closed his eyes and it wasn't about anger, the past, the Coopers. It was about a little girl named Darla McCormick. And it was about finding her safe. Amen to that.

Beth hitched her backpack on her shoulder. She had a first aid kit, water, snacks and a flare. She listened as the men planned. But she didn't want to stand around planning. She wanted to get on the road. She wanted to find Darla.

"Let's go, Bethlehem."

She looked up, met Jeremy's eyes. He smiled a real smile, not the teasing smile. "What?"

"We're a team. Didn't you hear Wyatt?"

"I was thinking." And obviously Wyatt wasn't thinking or he wouldn't have done that to her. He would have paired her with Jason. Or even Travis Cooper.

"Let's go. We're taking Wyatt's far twenty."

"Okay. Let me get my dog." She headed for Jason's truck and Jeremy was behind her.

"You're taking your dog?" Jeremy caught up with her.

"She's great at tracking. We couldn't find a calf last week and she led us right to him."

"Right, that isn't really tracking, it's just a dog that follows trails. And she's riding in my truck?" Jeremy pulled keys out of his pocket and held them up.

"You don't have to drive, I can." She had her own

truck, it was still there from earlier. They didn't even have to ride together.

"We can take the dog in my truck." Jeremy looked down at the collie and Beth smiled because the dog was already licking his hand and he reached to scratch it behind the ears. No one could resist… Well, the dog didn't even have a name yet. Everyone just called her "the dog."

Beth whistled and the dog followed her to Jeremy's truck. She opened the door and the dog hopped in, situating herself on the seat between them. Her pretty collie face broke into a smile. Jeremy opened his door, shook his head and climbed behind the wheel.

The collie whined and lay down, head on Beth's lap. Beth ran her hand over the fawn-colored head, sinking her fingers into thick, soft fur. She'd bathed the dog the previous evening and she still looked shiny and clean. Her limpid eyes stared up at Beth, seeking affection.

"What's the dog's name?" Jeremy pulled onto the road.

"She doesn't have a name."

"That's pretty sad, Beth. A dog should have a name."

"Do you have any ideas?"

"Yeah, Lucky."

"That's a horrible name. And it isn't a girl dog name. Why would you pick Lucky?"

He grinned. "It isn't as if you've come up with something better."

"Every stray shouldn't be named Lucky. I think she's a Petunia."

He laughed, white teeth flashing in his suntanned face. He glanced her way and then back to the road. The sun was going down and he took off his sunglasses. Beth hated that they were going to be searching in the dark. It would have been so much easier if they'd gotten started in daylight.

"You wouldn't do that to the dog." He shot her another look and then focused on the road. "Name it Petunia, I mean."

"Petunias are lovely flowers and they smell good."

"Fine, name the poor thing Petunia. But seriously, it sounds like a name for a pet skunk."

Silence washed over the cab of the truck for the next few minutes as they drove through town and into the country, past the Johnson ranch and down a dirt road to the back field that would put them in a direct path from where Darla had been walking in the direction the storm had traveled. Beth didn't want to think about that little girl getting picked up in that screaming vortex.

She wanted to believe that God would answer prayers and Darla would be found safe. She wanted to make deals with God. She would go to the mission field, or maybe give everything she had, if He'd help them find the child. But she knew better. She knew that God didn't need her promises or deals. She knew that prayer didn't work that way.

Jeremy parked. He glanced her way and she didn't want to get out of the truck. Fear knotted in her stomach. She looked out the window at the silent field, a breeze blowing the grass in waves. In the distance coyotes were yipping and howling. Darla was out there somewhere.

"Please help us find her," she whispered.

"In order for God to help us out, Beth, we need to start looking."

"I know." She opened her door and got out, stepping into the deep grass at the side of the road. Petunia hopped out of the truck behind her and followed her as she walked around the vehicle and met Jeremy. He had a .22 pistol in a holster at his side. She eyed the small-caliber handgun and he shrugged.

"You never know. A coyote, a snake, it pays to be prepared."

"Right." She'd grown up here. She knew that a person never knew what they'd encounter in a field, whether at night or during the day.

"We'll walk in the ditches first, down to the gate. One of us on either side. And then I think we should walk back and forth through the field. If we use the fence as a guide and go parallel from end to end we'll know we aren't skipping anything."

"Sounds like a good plan." Beth scanned the field, looking for anything out of the ordinary, anything remarkable. Nothing stood out. There was a hay barn and a crumbling foundation; leftovers from a forgotten farm.

They walked separately for a while, down the ditches on either side of the road. Beth felt choked with fear. What if they found Darla? What if they didn't? It was getting dark now. She wondered if Darla was afraid of the dark.

She met Jeremy at the gate to the pasture.

Jeremy reached for her hand. She hesitated, then accepted his strong hand holding hers tight.

"What did he do to you?" Jeremy's question was spoken in a soft voice as they walked along the fence line. They took careful steps in the dark and kept their attention focused on the ground, on clumps of weeds and brush that hadn't been cut down. The beams of their flashlights swung back and forth. The sun was now just a deep red glow in the dark violet evening sky.

"Jeremy, not now."

"Right, of course." He held tight to her hand. "I wish I could have stopped you that day. I wish I had gone to your dad and told him what you were planning."

She shook her head. "Stop."

Stop having a velvet-and-sandpaper voice that set her nerves on edge. Stop saying everything right.

She didn't want to have this conversation with Jeremy Hightree, a man who skated in and out of lives, who left broken hearts scattered like leaves in the fall. She'd already been broken. Now she was healing.

Her sense of self-worth had been stripped away, and she'd been putting herself back together piece by piece with the help of people who loved her and cared about her. It didn't make sense for Jeremy to be a part of the healing process.

So she kept walking and so did he. The dog stayed close, but always with her nose to the ground, sniffing, whimpering.

After an hour of walking back and forth across the field, Beth was starting to give up. She was starting to fear the worst. "Why don't you call and see if the others have had any luck?"

"They would have called us." He pulled his phone out anyway. Beth waited next to him.

Petunia ran ahead of them. Jeremy was dialing the phone, then suddenly Petunia was barking. The high-pitched yips filled the dark and silent night.

Chapter Six

"She found something."

Beth grabbed Jeremy's hand. Before he could slip the phone back into his pocket, Beth pulled him in the direction of the barking dog. Her flashlight beamed across the field, searching for the dog.

"It could be a skunk, Beth."

"I know, but it could be Darla."

Jeremy wanted to pull back, to tell her to calm down and to be realistic. An entire day had gone by and the girl hadn't been seen. If she were here, just a half mile from her home, why hadn't she gone home?

"I know what you're thinking." Beth slowed her headlong rush to get to the dog. The collie's barks had turned frantic and high-pitched. In the distance a coyote howled.

Jeremy's hand went to the gun that he'd slipped into the holster before he left the RV. It could be that the dog had a skunk cornered. It could be anything. Or anyone.

"Petunia. Dog," Beth called out in a quiet voice, "come here."

The dog continued to bark at the crawl space under the old foundation. That meant it was probably a rodent of some type. A skunk. Maybe a coon or opossum.

Or maybe the girl was there and prayers had been answered. He hoped prayers had been answered. He remembered years ago when Beth's mom had come to church, giving them all the news that nothing could be done. She'd fought for years but the battle with cancer had been lost. Her hair was gone. Her clothes hung on her body. She was ready to go home, but she would appreciate prayers. Maybe God would give her the healing the doctors hadn't. If not, she wanted peace.

And she'd left them. He'd been twelve and more angry than he'd ever been in his life. Beth's mom had been a mother to him. She'd left Beth alone.

He sucked in a breath, and Beth's hand touched his arm. He glanced down, unsure of what he should feel for the woman at his side.

He held the flashlight in one hand, Beth in the other. The dog was barking, loud, sharp barks. They reached the old homestead and the dog looked up at them but kept barking.

He leaned, crawling close to the hole in the foundation.

"Darla?" He waited. He could hear a scurrying sound. Just as he thought, rodents of some kind. One more time, though. "Darla, kiddo, people are looking for you."

And then a sob. He listened, making sure it wasn't Beth. The sound came from inside the crawl space. He couldn't fit through the hole. He flashed the light around the darkness, spotting rocks, old posts, concrete blocks. "Darla?"

"I'm calling for help." Beth was pushing buttons on her phone and then talking, asking for an ambulance, for support.

"Darla, you have to say something. Are you okay?"

"I'm here."

At the sound of her voice he exhaled a sigh. And he knew that one family would have a happy ending.

"Are you hurt?"

"My ankle." She sobbed again. "I want out of here. I just want to go home."

"Okay, now you have a light and we're going to get you home. Can you crawl toward me?"

He heard movement, rocks shifting, scraping. She cried out a little but she kept moving. And then he saw her, a dark-haired kid with big eyes in a pale face. There was a cut on her head. Blood had dripped down the side of her face and dried. Dirt smudged her cheeks.

"Darla, have you been sleeping? Or dizzy?"

She nodded a little. "I was running and something hit my head. I crawled under here, though. I knew about the old house because we play here sometimes."

"Good thing you knew that." He reached for her hand. Beth was behind him, her hand on his back, her face close to his. She trembled against him. His insides were jumbled together.

"I really want to go home." The child crawled out of the hole and into his arms. He sat back, holding her tight. Thin arms wrapped tight around his neck and held on. Beth's arms were around them both.

"Let's take a look and make sure you're okay." He set the girl on the foundation of the house. She had knobby knees and long legs.

"My ankle really hurts." She stretched her leg and he eased the shoe off her foot.

Next to him Beth was rummaging through that backpack of hers. She pulled out a bottle of water and a package of snack crackers. Jeremy stopped her from handing them over to the child.

"Nothing in your stomach hurts, right?" Jeremy held the child's shoeless foot and touched the swollen ankle. She flinched and then shook her head.

"My stomach is okay." Her big eyes were locked on the water and snacks that Beth still held. "I'm just really hungry."

He nodded and Beth handed the snacks to the child, first taking the lid off the water. She reached back into her pack and pulled out sterile wipes and bandages of all sizes. He grinned up at her. She was definitely prepared.

"I knew we'd find her." She smiled that beaming smile of hers.

"Right." A prayer answered. He was okay with prayers being answered for this girl and her family.

In the distance he heard sirens. The coyotes, silent for a moment, started in again. Their howls joined family dogs up and down this stretch of road. Darla shivered.

"It's okay," he said with a wink, and she smiled.

"They've been really close. I was afraid they would find me."

"I don't think they could have found you and they aren't real fond of people." He teased her with a grin and a wink, making her laugh.

Beth held out a sterile wipe. He handed her the flashlight and she held it up, giving him a clear look at the gash on the child's head. It was pretty deep and still oozing. He wiped at it, and Darla shuddered. Tears ran down her cheeks, turning dirt stains to mud.

"Sorry, kiddo, this might hurt but we need to clean this cut." He glanced back at Beth. "Do you have another bottle of water? We can wash it out for now and the paramedics can take care of the rest."

She handed him water. He tilted Darla's head to the side and rinsed the wound, wanting to get out the gravel and dirt embedded in the gash before he applied pressure to stop the bleeding. He wasn't a first aid expert, but he'd been around enough cowboys to know the basics.

Darla cried out when he pushed the gauze compress against the wound. "Hang in there. And think of all the stories you'll be able to tell the kids at school. You never know, you might even get interviewed by the newspaper."

That got her attention and she smiled. "Do you think?"

Lights flashed across the field from numerous vehicles lining up on the road next to the property. Someone must have opened the gate to the field because in moments the long line of cars, trucks and emergency vehicles were heading across the field. Jeremy shined the light to signal their location.

"They're almost here." Beth sat down next to the child, holding her close.

This night was nearly over. Jeremy needed distance. He needed to get his head on straight.

What had made him believe that coming to Dawson would be easy? He watched as Beth continued to talk in quiet whispers to the frightened child. When he'd planned this venture, the pros and cons of tearing down Back Street Church, he hadn't counted on Beth.

First responders and a half dozen others, probably including the girl's parents, were jumping out of vehicles and heading toward him. For a few minutes he could be distracted. His gaze shot back to Beth and Darla. Yeah, maybe not so distracted.

As the crowds pushed in, Beth lost track of Jeremy. She moved out of the way of the medical crew and the family members that were surrounding Darla. In the dark, with the dozens of people circling the area, it was easy to slip to the edge of the crowd, to watch and not be involved.

Her brother found her, though. He broke from the crowd and spotted her.

"You okay?" Jason slipped an arm around her shoulders and gave her a loose hug.

Beth nodded. "I'm good. Tired, though. This day has lasted forever."

"It has been a long day. You and Jeremy did good."

"Yeah." She watched Jeremy move, watched him stay in control. "What makes someone want to destroy something and yet, at the same time, go out of his way to keep someone safe?"

"It isn't about destroying the church, Beth." Jason shrugged. "It's about dealing with his past."

Yes, the past. No matter how much he said it was about building a business, the real motivation was Tim Cooper. He'd been an elder in the church, a pillar of the community, the man a kid like Jeremy would have admired. He would have wanted someone like Tim Cooper as a dad. And if things had been different, he would have been.

"Don't get that look in your eyes," Jason warned.

She smiled up at him. "It's dark, you can't see a look in my eyes. There isn't a look."

"Fixing him won't fix this problem. The church is still standing, Beth. Pray and give it time."

"I will." She watched the crowds surrounding people. "But I do have a plan and I'm not giving up."

"You called the historical society?"

"I did."

Jason sighed. "Beth, I know you want to save the church. I get that. But…"

"But what?"

"Nothing. I just don't want you hurt."

"I'm not going to get hurt."

"You're playing both sides of the fence."

Now what was that supposed to mean? "I'm not."

"Yeah, you are. You care about the church and you care about Jeremy Hightree. When push comes to shove, who are you going to choose?"

She didn't have an answer for him. Jason touched her shoulder. "Do you want to ride home with me?"

Beth watched as Darla was placed on the gurney, her mother holding her hand on one side, her dad on the other. "No, I'll ride back with Jeremy. We're parked down the road about a half mile."

Jeremy stood at the edge of the crowd, near Wyatt. He turned in her direction. As he approached, Jason gave one last warning. "Be careful."

"I will. I am."

"I'm heading back." Jeremy nodded at Jason as he spoke to her. Beth watched her brother, saw him bristle a little like their stock dog did when someone pulled up the drive.

Beth stood on tiptoe and kissed her brother's cheek. "I'll call when I get home."

"Make sure you don't forget." Jason hugged her, said something low, probably just a goodbye to Jeremy, and he left.

"It's always good to feel liked." Jeremy chuckled, the sound vibrating in the silence that followed the departure of the huge crowd that had been there just moments earlier. Taillights reflected shades of red as the long line of vehicles left single file, out of the field and then down the road. The lights on the ambulance flashed in the dark night.

They stood there for a long moment, the two of them alone again. Beth drew in a deep breath of clean night air. A light breeze blew around them, pushing the long grass in swirls and picking up leaves that had fallen from the trees during the storm. The storm that hit her heart at that moment rivaled the one that hit Dawson that day.

Had it only been a day? Was she really standing in this dark field with a sliver of moonlight cutting a path across the green grass and Jeremy Hightree standing in front of her, watching her?

Where was fear? She'd battled it for so long, she'd forgotten what it meant to be strong, to not worry about the next moment, the next day, the next crisis.

Jeremy tugged his hat low and smiled a smile so cute that everything she'd been thinking scattered like dandelion seeds in the wind. He stood in front of her, tall and strong and with hands that she knew were gentle. He was wearing a dark blue T-shirt. She still had his long sleeved shirt.

"Beth, are you okay?" His voice was soft but strong.

His eyes stayed with hers. Connected. She loved his eyes. They were warm caramel.

"I'm fine."

How long had they been standing there? Two minutes or five? Was he starting to wonder about her sanity? Her fingers curled into the palms of her hands. He stepped closer, his expression shifting from gentle to determined.

She closed her eyes. He touched her cheek and she looked up at him, at his cowboy smile that melted her down to her boots. He looked good in a cowboy hat. She felt warm in his shirt.

"It's been a long night." His words were drawn out, soft.

"It has."

"I'm going to hold you."

What did she say to that? Shivers of apprehension trickled down her spine. Apprehension or anticipation? She nodded a little.

"It wasn't an order, Beth. I thought that maybe we were both wrung out after this day."

He stepped close and his arms went around her, pulling her lightly against him, holding her close. She froze and started to pull back. His arms didn't lock around her. He didn't force her to stay. She didn't want to move.

"Holding you feels better than just about anything," he whispered near her ear. His cheek brushing hers was rough, his lips on her temple were warm.

She nodded and breathed deep. The fear and tension from the incredibly long day melted and she felt safe. It would take time to process that information. Jeremy Hightree made her feel safe.

"You okay?"

She nodded and instead of breaking the connection she moved farther into his embrace, into strong arms that held her close. She breathed deep and relaxed, her cheek against his shoulder.

"My legs are shaking," she admitted, holding tight, her hands on his arms.

"It was a long day and longer night. It's okay now."

She nodded into his chest. "Yeah."

When she looked up, his face was close to hers. Her lips parted on a sigh and she moved her hands up his arms to his shoulders. Jeremy pulled back, smiling.

"Not tonight, Beth."

She closed her eyes. No, not tonight. Her heart thudded, racing fast. Not tonight. Or tomorrow night. Not ever. What had she been thinking?

A soft embrace shouldn't distract her, but it had. Maybe Jason was right; she couldn't stand on both sides of this fence. Jeremy on one side, the church on the other.

She took his hand and they started across the field, toward the paved road where he'd parked his truck. She reminded herself that there was a dozer parked at the church, and tomorrow the historical society would be paying a visit to Back Street Church.

And Jeremy wasn't going to be happy.

Chapter Seven

Lunch was being served from tables set up on the front lawn of the church when an SUV bearing a county license plate pulled into the parking lot. Jeremy had eaten a sandwich that Vera pushed into his hand, while telling him that Chance Martin had rolled through town that morning. For whatever reason, Vera thought Jeremy should know.

It was going to be another long day on too little sleep. After watching Beth drive away the previous evening, he'd sat for hours on the glider outside his RV. Lights had glowed inside the church and he'd heard the soft murmur of voices as people settled in. He'd called his Tulsa dealership and asked his manager to get partitions out of storage and haul them to Dawson so the sanctuary could be divided.

As Jeremy crossed the lawn he eyed the dozer sitting on a trailer close to his RV and then his attention drifted to the group of people getting out of the SUV. Probably officials from the county or state emergency management team. He headed for his RV and his laptop. He was expecting a file from his partner, Dane Scott.

The group of people cut him off, stopping him at the edge of the parking lot. Two ladies and three men. Two of the men wore suits, one played it casual in dress slacks and a button-down shirt. They all had "official business" stamped on their smiling faces and Jeremy had an officially uneasy feeling in his gut.

"I'm not the guy in charge." Wyatt was in the church and he pointed them in that direction.

"Are you Jeremy Hightree?" the casually dressed guy asked.

"Yeah, that's me. I'm not in charge of the shelter, though. The man you need to talk to is Wyatt Johnson. He has names, family situations, all of the specifics."

"We're here about the church." One of the women stepped forward.

"Excuse me?"

Casual guy took over again. "Mr. Hightree, we received a nomination for this church to register it as a historical building."

Right, of course. He made eye contact with the balding man in a suit, the one who had yet to say a word. He was on the county planning and zoning commission, so Jeremy had seen him before. He should have expected this.

"What qualifications does the church meet to be registered as a historical building?" Jeremy had hoped to have a building started on this spot by now. Instead he was going to have to jump through small-town hoops.

"Well, sir, the church is one hundred years old."

"This is Oklahoma, a lot of buildings are that old. They can't all be deemed historical landmarks."

"Mr. Hightree, we are doing research on the building and how it came to be. This is only the beginning of our investigation."

"Right, so put me off and put off my business another few months. Maybe, if you're lucky, I'll get tired of waiting on you and walk away. But then this church will go back to being run-down and forgotten."

"We're just doing our job."

"Well, I have a job to do, too. I'm sure I'll hear from you soon." Jeremy walked around the group and into his RV.

When he walked out with the printout from his computer, they were gone. Kids were playing and a few people had set up lawn chairs under a tree. The men staying in the shelter had left right after lunch. Most of them had property that needed to be cleaned up, debris to haul off, and homes to rebuild or repair. A few of the people staying in the shelter just needed a place to stay until their electricity came back on.

One family had left already that morning. Someone had loaned them a generator.

Wyatt told him that there might be people in the shelter for a week, possibly two. Maybe by then the historical society would be done with their research.

The bike Jeremy was working on was in the barn. He walked across the road and opened the barn door. One of the horses he'd brought with him walked from the corral into the open stall to watch, and probably hope for grain. He'd been fed a few hours ago, so the gelding was out of luck.

He rolled the bike out of the stall and into the center aisle of the barn. Working on the motorcycle would help him clear his thoughts. That's how he'd started in this line of work. While he'd been recovering from the broken femur and torn-up knee, he'd built a bike for himself, then for a friend. It had been good therapy during his rehab. Within a year it had become a business that kept him busy. And then it had become a business that kept several guys busy.

With the motorcycle in front of him he could pretend that the only thing he had to worry about was building the perfect bike. The perfect chrome for the fenders. The perfect paint job. He straddled the seat and reached for the handlebars. The handlebars had to be perfect, just the right height for his customer. A custom bike was just that, custom. Every inch of it was designed specifically for the person who ordered it.

A truck came up the road. He glanced out the wide double doors and watched as Beth pulled in. She had parked in the church parking lot and as she got out she waved at the two little boys playing with toy fire trucks. She ruffled the blond hair of one boy and high-fived the other.

He climbed off the bike and reached for a rag to wipe his hands. But he sure wasn't going to go rushing across the road to follow her around the way the kids at the church were doing. He had a little self respect.

Not a lot, obviously, because he was definitely thinking of excuses for heading back over to the church.

His attention drifted to the leveled house. Working on it would keep him busy and keep his mind off the one thing he hadn't been able to shake since yesterday—the way it felt to hold Beth. He walked the short distance across the field to the foundation that was all he had left of a house. He picked up a few boards, nails jutting out, and tossed them on a pile of debris.

The best way to clean was probably to pile up the

wood and burn it. He'd try to salvage what wasn't broken into pieces or splintered. Maybe he'd put the good wood in a pile for anyone who needed it for small repairs.

A truck pulled into the drive next to the house. Jackson Cooper stepped out, waving and then turning back to the truck. When he turned back toward Jeremy he was pulling on leather work gloves.

"Need some help?" Jackson picked up a few loose boards on his way over.

"Not really."

Jackson laughed and continued to pick up boards. "Too bad. Everyone is getting a helping hand. You're included in that."

"I think we should concentrate on people who really need to get their homes back in order. This is just a frame, or was. I have a place to live."

"Yeah, well, we have to start somewhere, right?"

Did he mean as family, or did he mean start somewhere on the house? Jeremy let it go, which wasn't easy for him.

"I guess so."

"I heard about the historical society paying you a visit."

Jeremy threw a board onto the growing pile of usable lumber. "Word travels fast in a small town."

"Yeah, it does. You had to know someone would do something like that."

"I guess I hadn't really considered it." But now he knew that everyone had a story about Back Street. Today one of the families using it as a shelter had told him about their wedding. Twenty years ago they had walked down the aisle at Back Street. Eighteen years ago their son was dedicated and later baptized at Cooper Creek.

"Remember when we carved our names under the back pew?"

Jeremy threw a few splintered boards into the burn pile and walked away. Jackson tossed another question at him. Jeremy turned. "I remember."

Jackson grinned at him. "Kind of gets you right here," he slapped his heart, "doesn't it?"

"Yeah, that's where it gets me."

And coming across the road was Beth Bradshaw.

She was a complication that he hadn't planned on. He'd honestly thought he'd get this done before anyone really noticed what was happening. He hadn't expected Dawson to have a planning and zoning commission. He hadn't planned on permits and signatures. He really hadn't thought that anyone would care.

He looked past her to the faded church. Two days ago he'd seen an eyesore that no one should miss. Today he saw a place where lives were changed. The stories he'd been told were fresh in his mind, pushing his own story aside because the other stories weren't as painful.

Jackson walked up and slapped him on the back, hard enough to knock him forward a step. "You might want to get that look on your face under control, little brother."

"There's no look on my face."

"Yeah, there is. It's the 'end of the road' look a guy gets when all of a sudden being single doesn't seem like so much fun. So what, you've dated senator's daughters and heiresses. Nothing compares to a cowgirl with cherry lip gloss and a smile like that."

"I have to go."

Jackson shrugged and pulled off his gloves. "Me too. I'll be back later to help you clean up this mess.

Might want to put on some aftershave and take her to dinner."

"You might want to stop playing big brother."

"No, I don't think so. This is kind of fun."

Jeremy shook his head and walked away. Fun wasn't the word he would have used for his relationship with Jackson. But then again, it wasn't all bad. Beth walked up the driveway. Her smile was shy and he was always surprised how it made him want to take care of her. She made him want to be an Old West cowboy, the kind of guy that tossed his jacket on a mud puddle for the woman to step on to keep her feet dry.

On top of that pile of emotion was something else he had to deal with.

"You called the historical society?"

She nodded. He had hoped she'd deny it. Instead she came right out and admitted her guilt, or at least her part in trying to stop his plans.

"You brought in a dozer." She countered with a little shrug of slim shoulders.

"Yeah, I did." He watched Jackson get in his truck and back down the drive. Jackson tipped the brim of his hat and laughed.

"I'm sorry, Jeremy, but I had to do something. This seemed like the only answer. This church has been here for a long time. If it gets registered as an historical building I can get grants to help maintain it."

"Beth, is it really about money? People in this town could have come together and done something."

"I think that time goes by and we all get used to the way things are and think that nothing will change. We didn't know that the trust for the Gibson land, this land, had a limit and that if the church wasn't used would

revert back to their family. The kids who inherited
live in Kansas City. They didn't care about a church in
Dawson."

"Well, plenty of people care now." His phone buzzed
and he pulled it out of his pocket. "Sorry, I have to take
this."

She nodded and walked away. He watched her go
as he answered the phone. She knew how to twist a
guy inside out, and he didn't think she realized she was
doing it. He'd just about give her anything if he could,
but he couldn't let go of his plans for the church.

He thought about the look in her eyes last night, when
she'd been in his arms smiling up at him. He tried to
block images of how she'd look at him when the church
was gone.

As Beth crossed the road, Angie Cooper pulled into
the parking lot. Beth shot a look over her shoulder and
saw Jeremy walk back into the barn. He had to have
seen Angie, and of course he was going to ignore her.

Beth had other things on her mind today, other plans
to put into action. If the historical society couldn't stop
Jeremy, she had a plan B. She would get signatures and
go to planning and zoning commission with a petition
to stop the building of a commercial business inside
Dawson. She'd been doing research and there wasn't a
current ordinance to stop Jeremy, but that didn't mean
she couldn't try to get one put on the books.

She stopped at her truck and grabbed the clipboard
and pen she'd brought with her. When she turned, Angie
Cooper was standing behind her. Beth wanted to be
Angie someday. A doctor's daughter from Oklahoma
City, Angie always managed to look put together. She

was cool under pressure. Her clothes were never wrinkled and her shoes always worked.

How did a person get to be Angie Cooper? Maybe because she'd survived. Angie had survived a dozen kids. She had survived learning that Tim Cooper was Jeremy Hightree's father. Some said she had always suspected.

"How is he?" Angie waited for Beth to close the truck door and fell in next to her as they walked toward the church.

"He?"

"Jeremy? This can't be easy for him, coming home after so many years, and now this."

Why would Angie ask her about Jeremy's well-being? "I think he's okay."

Or he was until she'd turned the historical society loose on him. And how would he be when he saw the petition? She swallowed misgivings.

"What is that?" Angie indicated the clipboard with a nod of her head.

"It's a petition. I'm going to try to stop him from doing this."

Angie looked at the church and sighed. "I'm not sure if that's the best thing to do, Beth."

"Why wouldn't it be? This church is a part of our community. We can't walk away from it and let him do this."

Angie slipped an arm around Beth's waist. "People have reasons for doing what they do, Beth. From the outside it looks like he's doing this for the wrong reasons. But it isn't all about the past. We all work through our anger in different ways."

The biggest reason to be like Angie Cooper, she was a forgiving woman. She was a class act.

"He'll regret this."

"Maybe, but we learn from our regrets. We learn to do better the next time."

Beth realized she had a long way to go before she would be like Angie Cooper. "I know you're right."

Angie laughed a little. "But you're still going to stand between Jeremy and this church."

"If I have to tie myself to the porch to keep him from dozing it down, I will."

A few minutes later she was explaining the petition to the Johns family and they were signing it. Of course Jeremy would pick that minute to walk into the church. He walked down the aisle, toward her and then with a shake of his head he turned back toward the door.

Beth followed him out the door, where he stopped at the top of the steps. He stared straight ahead, giving her only his unshaven profile and strong jaw to look at. When she reached him, he shook his head a little and looked down at her.

"Beth, do you have to be the one doing this?"

"I'm sorry."

He shook his head and walked down the steps. "I'm sure you are. If anyone asks, tell them Scrooge is helping the Matheson family clean up their farm."

"Jeremy, I am sorry."

He walked across the churchyard, stopping to talk to one of the little boys playing under the oak tree.

Beth watched him leave and she held on to the clipboard knowing that some things you couldn't take back.

Chapter Eight

The Matheson farm had taken a pretty hard hit. Jeremy stood next to the pile of debris that had been a barn and shook his head. People around here didn't let a little thing like losing everything chase them off from their homes and the town they'd grown up in.

Since he'd been born and raised here, he knew a thing or two about standing his ground. He regretted that it had to be Beth he came up against in this battle. When he thought about Bethlehem Bradshaw he remembered her in his shirt, her in his arms. Now he had the image of her with that stupid clipboard full of names.

He pulled his gloves back on and grabbed the wheelbarrow he'd been using to cart old shingles and pieces of metal that were scattered around the yard. A chainsaw buzzed in the background as the trees that had been toppled were cut up.

He'd give this job another hour and then he needed to head for Tulsa where he still had a business that needed his attention. He had three custom bikes going out next month and a dealership that was receiving a shipment of new bikes next week.

The other thing he needed to do was talk to his lawyer about the trouble brewing with the building. That didn't sit well with him. Yeah, he wanted the business built on a site that already had utilities, water and septic, but he wasn't interested in a legal battle that would tear the community apart.

As long as the church served as a shelter, he had time to think about what he should do and how to move forward. For the most part, people were thankful that he had opened Back Street as a shelter.

Reese Cooper had slapped him on the back earlier and told him that it meant a lot to the community.

He rounded the corner and Ryder Johnson jumped out of the way. He raised his hands and grinned. "Watch out, it wasn't me."

Jeremy tried to smile. "Well then you're probably the only one."

Ryder walked with him to the pile of debris that they'd burn after everything was cleaned up. "It's been a rough couple of days in good old Dawson."

"Yeah, it has." And they weren't going to talk about the church. Jeremy would have said thank you, but that would have brought it up. "Did Rob Matheson get an appointment in Grove?"

"Yeah, he headed that way about two hours ago. It'll probably take all day, but he has to do something. He didn't have insurance on his tractor. The insurance on the barn won't cover what was inside it."

"That's a tough break."

"It is. He's in a mess of trouble if he doesn't get temporary funds to keep him going."

"We might have to do some kind of fundraiser to help out the folks in town who don't have enough insurance to cover everything." Jeremy had talked to Wyatt about the same thing.

"Yeah, that's what Wyatt said. Maybe the idea of a rodeo would work."

"Might, if we can get participation from outside Dawson. Wyatt is going to work on it."

Ryder pulled gloves out of his pocket. "I'm going to get back to work. Sara is on her roof over there, nailing down tarps. Their kid is helping, but I think he's only ten."

Jeremy followed the direction of Ryder's gaze. Sure enough Sara Matheson had climbed up on the roof of her old farmhouse. She had blue tarps stretched over the roof that covered the back rooms of her house.

"Later, Ryder."

Ryder nodded and walked off. Jeremy went back to work with the wheelbarrow.

After hauling a few more loads from the house to the burn pile, Jeremy pulled off his leather gloves and headed for the table that had been set up with cold drinks and coffee. He poured himself a paper cup of sweet tea and took a long drink.

Vera walked over to stand across the table from him. The owner of the Mad Cow seemed to be everywhere, helping everyone.

"Vera, I don't know how you do it all."

She took his cup and refilled it. "You do what you have to do, Jeremy. You know that. We know how to survive here in Dawson. We've been through more than one tornado. We've been through more than one crisis. Folks always find a way to bounce back."

"Yeah, but you're giving away more than you're taking in right now."

"Now, Jeremy, you know that God will take care of me. He always has. Remember when my house burned down years ago? My neighbors were there before the fire trucks. They helped me clean up and rebuild."

"Yeah, I remember." He hadn't been very old, maybe thirteen. He and some of the boys in town had helped her out at the Mad Cow for a few days after the fire.

Vera winked and handed him a sandwich. "Most of us understand about the church, Jeremy. We don't want it gone, but we understand."

He hadn't expected that at all. Sara Matheson walked up though, ending the conversation.

"You doing okay, Sugar?" Vera poured Sara a cup of iced tea.

"We're going to make it, Vera." Sara took the tea and smiled at Jeremy. "Thanks for all your help today."

"I'm sorry you all got hit this hard."

She'd shrugged it off but a tear trickled down her cheek. She brushed it away and smiled. "It could have been worse, Jeremy. We weren't here. None of us were hurt. I even found my wedding ring. Actually, Wyatt found it in the yard this morning."

"I'm glad to hear that." Jeremy tossed his cup in the trash. "I'm going to get more work done before I have to leave. Let me know if you need anything."

As he walked away, Jackson followed him, his hat pulled low and dirt streaking the front of his T-shirt. Once, years ago, they'd been told they looked like brothers. At sixteen, Jeremy had laughed and said he wasn't near as ugly as Jackson.

But when he'd looked in the mirror that night, he'd seen what that other person had been talking about. It had spooked him back then, made him wonder things about the dad he'd never known, the guy his mom had told him had just been passing through.

It had been tough, growing up, being the man of the house from the time he could pull on his own boots. It had been tough, trying to model himself after men in the community that he'd looked up to, men like Tim Cooper. Man, he'd been modeling himself after his own dad.

"This is a mess." Jackson picked up a piece of sheet metal and tossed it in the wheelbarrow Jeremy pushed across the lawn.

"Yeah, it is."

"Dad wants to talk to you."

Jackson as the family messenger. Jeremy would have put Blake, the older, more mature Cooper in that role. Jackson, though, he was easy to talk to. Blake had his own life, his own problems.

"Nah, I don't think I want to do that." Jeremy toed his boot into the dirt and looked off to the west.

"You should. This isn't going away, Jeremy."

At that, he laughed. "The only thing that doesn't seem to be going away is you. Every time I turn around you're there. It's getting kind of old."

Jeremy started to walk away. A hand grabbed his arm and stopped him. He turned, looked at the hand that held him without giving. He shook loose but Jackson didn't back off.

"Jackson, I don't need more history lessons. I'm tired of the past."

"Then why are you acting like you're still living there?"

"I didn't think I was until I came back here and found out how much you people hold on to it."

Jackson grinned big. "Yeah, we do have a thing for

holding on to the past. Most of us don't have a dozer aimed at a church."

"When did you start caring about church, or about what happened to Back Street?"

Jackson shrugged. "I never stopped caring about church. I went all my life. I guess I kind of figured I had it handled. I'm okay with God. And that church didn't do a thing to you."

"No, it didn't."

"Have a talk with him, Jeremy."

"Right, I'll think about that." And he'd think about jumping in front of Jim Pritchard's big black Angus bull, too. Never.

Jackson slapped him on the back. "You know how I know you're a Cooper?"

"How's that?"

"That stubborn streak. Yeah, that's Cooper through and through. No way can you possibly be wrong. Am I right?"

"I guess so, you're a Cooper."

Jeremy walked off with Jackson's amused laughter ringing in his ears. He tried not to think about growing up alone when he'd had brothers just a mile down the road. Jackson, Reese, Blake, Travis and Jesse. Yeah, it would have been nice to be a part of their lives.

Stubborn. Yeah, that stubborn streak was a mile wide.

Wyatt Johnson, present at nearly every cleanup Jeremy found himself at, turned from the foundation that had been a barn until just a few days ago. Jeremy wondered how the guy did it all.

"Jeremy, how's it going at Back Street?" Wyatt stepped back and stood next to Jeremy.

"I imagine as well as can be expected. What about you, Wyatt? Burning the candle at both ends, aren't you?"

Wyatt grinned. "Both ends and in the middle."

"Don't you have a pretty new wife at your house?"

"Yeah and I couldn't do this without her."

"What, run a ranch, pastor a church and tend to the entire town of Dawson like it's one of your kids?"

Wyatt didn't seem bothered by the observation. He shrugged, still smiling. "This is our community, Jeremy. And you feel the same way. If you didn't, you wouldn't be doing everything to help out."

Jeremy turned to watch the group of men, a few women and even kids that had showed up for this cleanup at the Matheson farm. There was a list at the church. Each home or business that needed help was on the list and volunteers signed up to be there.

"Yeah, this is our town."

Wyatt laughed. "Isn't that a country song? Isn't there something about a girl whose name he painted on the water tower?"

"I never painted anyone's name on a water tower." Never. And it had never bothered him before. Today, for whatever crazy reason, it did.

His heart felt kind of like a lonely old dog left on the side of the road. He laughed. That wasn't a country song, but probably should be.

"I think I'm going to take a drive."

Wyatt tipped the brim of his hat. "Don't be climbing no water towers, Jeremy."

"Why, are you the town cop on top of everything else?" Jeremy managed a smile and even laughed a little at the idea of Wyatt with a badge and a Bible.

"Nope, not the town cop. But I know the guy who will take you down if you hurt his sister."

"Yeah, I'm not planning on going there."

But on the way through Dawson his eyes did stray to the old gray metal water tower. He grinned, remembering Wyatt's words and the reality that he'd never painted anyone's name on anything. He'd never thought about settling down.

And yet, he had a strange urge to buy a can of spray paint on his way out of town.

Jeremy had been gone for two days. Not that Beth kept track of his whereabouts, but the RV had been strangely quiet. A town that had been without him for several years now seemed quiet and lonely without him there.

Beth knew that her actions might have driven him away. Maybe not permanently, but at least for a few days. The historical society was still researching Back Street Church and the planning and zoning committee were looking into zoning for commercial businesses. The wheels were all set in motion and Beth regretted her part in it.

Beth spent day three after the tornado delivering sandwiches to work crews in the area and to families that were toughing it out in damaged homes with no electricity. It had turned hot and humid, making it more miserable for everyone involved.

She had turned off the main road onto a dirt road that led down to the creek where she'd spent a lot of her childhood playing in the cold, clear water. It would feel good, to take off her shoes and wade in the creek, to forget everything going on in Dawson.

She parked her truck in the grassy clearing and pulled the keys out of the ignition. As she walked down the trail a tiny shard of apprehension slid through her middle. Or maybe it was common sense telling her to be careful. She walked a little farther and stopped. The creek bubbled along, a rushing, energetic sound. In the distance she heard the steady hum of a tractor engine and on the road the crunch of tires on gravel.

She walked a little farther, closer to the creek, deeper into the woods. The air was cooler and a soft breeze rustled the leaves in the trees. When she reached the creek she leaned against a tree to kick off her shoes.

The sound of shattering glass stopped her. Birds flapped over head and flew among the branches of the trees.

Beth froze, her breath holding in lungs that refused to cooperate. The sound of metal and glass. And then the sound of a vehicle starting and racing off.

Her legs shook and refused the order to run.

She couldn't run back to her truck. What if someone was still up there? What if it hadn't been her truck, hadn't been what she thought? Maybe someone had been in a wreck? Or perhaps tossed something out a window?

But no matter what, she couldn't force herself to walk back up the path. She was frozen in that spot, stuck in the past and in memories of Chance's abuse.

The old Beth stood there, afraid to move, afraid of what he'd do next. It had been that way for so many years. Always the fear of what would push him to lose his temper.

She edged down the path, to a spot that allowed her a clear view of her truck and the reality that someone had indeed been there, and she had been the target. The windows were cracked and splintered. A dent creased the door of the truck.

What now? She wasn't going to cower. She wasn't going to cry. She was going to be the new Beth, the one that took charge of her life. The one who didn't shake in her shoes. If only she could convince her legs of that fact.

For a long moment she stood on the shadowy path, surrounded by trees and things that scurried in the fallen leaves. She listened for the return of the car or truck that had driven away. Whoever it had been probably wouldn't return. But she wasn't going out on that road, either.

The creek sparkled, clear and cool. She had wanted to wade in the water, to cool off the way she had when she'd been a kid. Instead she remained on the path and kept walking. Several hundred feet down the trail she slipped through strands of sagging barbed wire.

The sound of the tractor she'd heard earlier was louder now. The field she was walking through belonged to the Coopers. Ahead of her, probably another ten or fifteen minutes of walking, was Back Street. She could make it to the church and someone would give her a ride.

She slipped through another fence, onto the land Jeremy Hightree had purchased months ago. The grass had been cut and was drying in the warm sun. He must have decided to bale it for hay.

The sweet smell of clover brought back so many memories of childhood picnics and playing in the field. She walked a little slower, feeling a little calmer now. She was close to people, close to help.

Ahead of her the tractor circled. The grass, nearly two

feet high, fell beneath the blade of the mower. Tomorrow or the next day he'd rake the hay into rows to bale. She looked up, searching for clouds. Rain always put a damper on hay season. Grass had to be dried before it could be baled.

The big, green tractor turned the corner. She kept walking but the tractor slowed and stopped. Beth waved and Jeremy waved back. And then she realized he was motioning her in his direction. She glanced to the south, saw the steeple of Back Street Church. She shifted her gaze back to the tractor and to Jeremy.

She remembered him sitting in the park all of those years ago, telling her to be careful, to rethink her decision to leave town with Chance. He'd told her then that he'd give her a ride home. She could pretend it never happened.

She could no longer pretend. Chance had happened. Her life with him had happened.

The image of her truck at the side of the road, glass shattered and a dent in the door, reminded her that Chance could still control her life. Even if he hadn't done that to her truck, the fear she'd felt, the memories it had brought back, were because of Chance.

She turned in the direction of the tractor. Thirty feet away from her it stopped, and Jeremy opened the door. He stepped out, his ball cap pushed back, giving her a full view of his face, the full effect of his smile. The white T-shirt made his tan look deeper, darker. His teeth flashed white in a smile that nearly made her stop and rethink this decision.

She was running to safety and for a moment it felt like anything but.

"You're pale." He reached down and pulled her up. "Where's your truck?"

Beth glanced back toward the road. From the perch on top of the tractor she could see Back Street. She could see the church and the cars in the parking lot.

"Bethlehem?"

She slid into the cab of the tractor. It was cool in there and Jeremy pulled the door closed, capturing them in the tinted interior where the radio played a Brad Paisley song and the engine of the tractor idled, vibrating the big machine.

"Someone trashed my truck. I parked to walk down to the creek and someone pulled up and vandalized it."

"What the…"

She bit down on her bottom lip and wished the tears away. His expression softened and his arms slid around her waist. Holding her close.

"You're okay?" His voice trickled down her spine like warm water. And then it wasn't a question, it was reassurance. "Beth, you're okay."

She nodded. The tractor wasn't meant for two so she had to sit close. His arm around her waist held her on the narrow seat.

"We need to call the police." He pointed the tractor in the direction of his barn and shifted gears.

"No."

"No?"

He braked and the big machine rumbled to a halt.

"Jeremy, I don't want to start this over again. I'm here. Chance is in California. But I don't want this to be my life."

"He's in Dawson."

Jeremy's words shook her from the daze she'd been in. "How do you know?"

"Someone saw him drive through town."

"Maybe he didn't do it."

"You really think that?"

She glanced out the gray tinted window at the half mowed field. "I don't want my life to be about police reports and fear."

"Then do something about it. Don't let him bully you. You need to make it clear to him that you're not afraid."

"But I am."

"Beth, he hurt you. He was a coward who took you across the country so you wouldn't have anyone to turn to. You're not that girl anymore. You're stronger than that. You have family and friends who will back you up."

More regret. "I can't believe you're even talking to me after what I've done to you."

Jeremy leaned close and he smiled, "Yeah, so am I. You're going to end up costing me a lot of money because I am going to fight this."

"I know." She wiped a finger under her eyes. "And I'm sorry."

"But it's a battle you have to fight. I get that."

The tractor lumbered forward. He steered with one hand on the wheel. His other arm was around her, keeping her next to him. A few minutes later he parked the tractor next to the barn.

They sat for a second. Jeremy's arm was still around her. She closed her eyes and leaned against his shoulder. It felt good there, with his arm around her. It felt safe.

"Jeremy, thank you."

"For what?" he whispered. His breath was soft. His lips brushed close to her ear.

"For being my friend."

His arm tightened. He took off his hat and dropped it on the gearshift. He brushed his hand across her cheek, rough and gentle at the same time.

"Beth, you're beautiful. Stubborn but beautiful."

He leaned, holding her close. She touched his shoulder, afraid to breathe, afraid to interrupt the moment. Her heart had been waiting for this, longing for it. His lips brushed her temple first, and then her cheek while his right hand cradled the back of her head.

When his lips touched hers, tears slid down her cheeks. His lips on hers were tender, forcing old memories from her mind and replacing them with something new and wonderful. Her heart soared, reaching for his. This kiss took her back and suddenly she was sixteen again, standing on the creek bank with a boy who wanted to be a rodeo star.

That kiss had been the kiss of a boy. This time she was being held by a man, a man who made her feel everything all at once, and beautiful. His arms held her close and his lips were firm, sweeping her away from reality and into a world where she believed in fairy tales again.

And then he pulled away, too soon.

He touched his forehead to hers. "I don't want to be the next person to hurt you. And I don't want the church between us this way."

"What?" Her voice shook. A moment like this shouldn't end with words that sounded like him putting distance between them.

"You deserve someone safe, someone who isn't going to hurt you."

"You mean the church?"

"The church, yeah. And me. Beth, you deserve someone steady."

"Right, of course." She slid from his embrace. Standing, she reached for the door of the tractor. Lights flashed in the corner of her eye.

"The police are here. Someone probably spotted your truck."

She nodded and opened the door to step out. "I have to go."

"Let me park this thing and I'll go with you."

She smiled back at him. "I can handle it."

She had to handle it because she had drawn the line between them and he had drawn another line. She walked toward the church and wondered how it had become the battleground.

If she had to choose between Back Street and Jeremy…

She wouldn't let herself think that thought, not now. A deputy was getting out of a patrol car and her truck had been vandalized. That should be enough to think about for one day.

Chapter Nine

Jeremy parked the tractor and hopped down, landing hard on his left leg. Big mistake. He winced, inhaling a deep breath, pushing past the jarring pain. As a kid he'd been told all of those falls from horses, and the bull wrecks, would catch up with him. In the last couple of years he'd become a believer.

His injuries were catching up with him. He was starting to feel like an old man. He watched the retreating back of Bethlehem Bradshaw. Other things were catching up with him, too. He grinned at that thought and even laughed a little. He'd played pretty fast and loose over the years, thinking he'd never get caught.

But she wasn't the type of woman a man walked away from. She was the type of woman a guy had kids with, maybe a minivan. Or a big old SUV, the kind with three rows of seats and movie screens that dropped down from the ceiling.

If he'd been a settling-down kind of guy, it would have been with someone like Beth.

He limped across the road to the church. A crowd had gathered. Jason had arrived; so had Beth's dad.

They were standing with her as she spoke to the deputy. Jeremy walked to the back of the group and waited. He listened as Beth explained what had happened.

He listened when the deputy told her that Chance was in town visiting his family. Of course that wasn't enough to charge the guy. If she'd seen a vehicle, or there had been witnesses... There hadn't been.

Jeremy watched the color drain from Beth's face, saw her glance around, looking for something or someone. Her gaze latched on to his. He smiled and winked. He didn't know if he could convey in a look that he wouldn't let anyone hurt her, but he hoped she understood.

He would do his best to keep her safe from Chance. He wouldn't be the one to hurt her, either. And he didn't know if she really got that message. She needed someone better than him. She needed a man who planned to stick around, not a cowboy who had never held on to a woman long enough to get attached.

He walked back to his RV and eased his way up the steps. Man, he was tired of living in two rooms. He had a big house on the outskirts of Tulsa. If he'd been there he'd have taken a swim to work the kinks out of his leg.

Instead he grabbed a bottle of water out of the fridge and opened the lid on a bottle of aspirin. A few of those and putting his leg up for a minute, he'd be as good as new. Or as good as he was going to get.

He walked past the door and glanced out. Beth was talking to her dad. She wiped at her cheeks and looked away. She looked in his direction again. He was the last person she needed to look toward. Man, he'd hurt more women than he could remember. He wasn't anyone's hero.

The Bible on the table caught his attention. He sat down in the half-size recliner and kicked back, his legs stretched out on the footstool. He set his bottle of water on the table and picked up that Bible.

"Yeah, I remember." He remembered being a kid in secondhand clothing two sizes too small and coming to Back Street to feel safe.

He remembered taking his Sunday school lessons so seriously he would've fought anyone who teased him for going to church.

His stories were a lot like the ones that people had shared with him. People's pasts were connected to Back Street Church. His own past was connected to this church.

This morning there had been a message on his cell phone from the head of planning and zoning. They had a list of names on a petition, people who were asking that the land the church was on not be zoned for commercial use.

That was Beth's handiwork. He kind of admired her pluck, even if it was going to cost him a bundle to fight it.

A knock on the door interrupted those thoughts. He put the Bible down and looked up. Beth peeked in through the screen.

"What's up?"

She stood on the outside looking in at him. "Nothing. Are you coming out?"

"Yeah, in a sec." As soon as he could convince himself to put the footstool down. "You can come in."

She opened the door. "You're sitting still? In the middle of the day."

He nodded in the direction of the kitchen. "Grab a bottle of water if you want."

She did and then she turned, her face still a little pale. Her eyes huge and rimmed with dark smudges. "They're going out to talk to him. It'll make him mad."

"Beth, that's how he controls you, by making you believe you have no power."

Should he remind her that they were in a battle over Back Street and yet here she was in his RV? No, he wouldn't, because she needed someone to talk to.

She sat down on the sofa. "I know. I do know that. But it isn't easy being strong. If I turn him in, he threatens to do worse when he gets out. If I call the police, he makes me feel guilty. How can I do that to someone I love?"

"Do you love him?" He thought his voice sounded strained.

Beth opened her water. She didn't look up. And he had a long minute of wondering why she had to think about the answer to that question. Finally she shook her head. He pretty near sighed with relief.

"No, I don't love him. I think he killed any love I had for him a long time ago. The only thing left is fear, and I'm working on that."

"You're a lot stronger than you think. You walked away."

She smiled, her expression soft. "I stayed. For a long time, I stayed."

"I know.

"He had me convinced that I wasn't worth anything. He made me believe that no one would want me but him, and that I was lucky to have him."

Jeremy forced himself to relax, to take a deep breath

and unclench his fists. He put the footstool down and leaned forward, because he couldn't sit back and have this conversation with her. He wasn't worth much, but he'd never hurt a woman the way Beth had been hurt.

"Beth, he's a sick individual with a big problem. And you aren't the cause. Man, any guy would be lucky—no, blessed—to have you."

She smiled one of those smiles that knocked a guy backward. It hit him full force. It made him want to stand in front of her, protecting her forever. It made him want to jump in his truck and drive over to the Martin place.

He tried hard not to think that he'd just said blessed. God talk felt like a foreign language. But what else could he say, other than the truth?

Beth's smile dissolved a little. She held the bottle of water in both hands and looked up.

"Jeremy, I've been to counseling. For the last year I've had to work through those feelings. Chance tore at my self-esteem to keep me a prisoner in our relationship. I've been rebuilding myself, my faith, my life." She stood up. "And now I'm going to get you a bag of ice."

"Ice?"

"For whatever you injured jumping out of that tractor. I saw you limping across the road like some old dog that had been hit and was coming home to lick his wounds."

"It's my knee and the pins holding my leg together. Too bad they don't have bionic parts, I'd be worth millions."

"They wouldn't put bionic parts in a cowboy that can't stay off the back of a bull." She laughed, "Or *stay on* the back of a bull. I guess that's where the problems start, when you fall off."

"Thanks."

"Don't mention it." She opened a drawer and found a plastic bag. After she dumped a tray of ice in it she brought it back and dropped it on his knee.

"Thanks." He winced and moved the ice. "I really don't need it. I took aspirin."

"You can take care of yourself, right?"

"I'm a long way on the other side of fifteen, Beth."

"So am I." She kneeled next to him. "Don't take over. Promise me you won't do that. I need to be strong."

He tangled his fingers in brown hair that slipped through his fingers like strands of lavender-scented silk. She leaned and he brushed the back of his hand against her cheek. Soft. He sighed and pulled his hand back, because this wasn't where they needed to be going.

She needed to be strong. That was her way of warning him to step carefully and to not invade her life.

"I know that you're strong." He also knew that if he caught Chance Martin anywhere near her, Jeremy wouldn't be responsible for what he did to the other man.

He would let her be strong. He wouldn't let her get hurt. Not even by him.

Beth stood and then she leaned to kiss Jeremy on the cheek. It should have been an easy gesture between two people who had known each other since childhood. An innocent kiss on the cheek. But she paused in the moment, breathing in his scent, his warmth. His hand moved, to her neck and he held her there, her lips against his cheek, her breath catching and then releasing in a quick sigh. He turned and their lips connected.

But she was being strong, not afraid. She was in control of her life. She was in control of this kiss, her heart melting, her world spinning. She opened her eyes and released herself from his grasp. As she stepped back, he stood, still holding her hand.

He looked apologetic. Oh, no, that wasn't what she wanted. She touched her finger to his lips.

"Don't say it. Please don't say how sorry you are. Remember, rebuilding self-esteem here."

He grinned. And he didn't say anything.

Beth backed toward the door. "I'm going home now. Jason is taking me, since my truck is unfortunately out of commission."

"Jason is out there? Waiting for you? He knows you're in here?"

The questions came fast and she laughed at the way his eyes darted to the door. "Yeah, he's out there. He gave me five minutes and said if I'm not back he's coming in."

"Oh…"

"Don't say a bad word."

He shot her a look and ran a hand through hair that was a little spiky on top. She should let him off the hook, but what fun would that be?

"Beth, seriously, I respect Jason. You're…"

"Off limits? Haven't I always been? Wasn't that the problem when I was sixteen? My dad caught us together. Jason made a threat against your person. You were a chicken."

"I'm a lot of things but…"

"But you're not a chicken? Really?"

He took a step toward her, barely grimacing, she noticed. His brown eyes glinted in the shadowy interior of the RV. She didn't smile, wouldn't smile. Her heart had needed this, had needed him. And she wasn't going to think about the past, or why he was there.

"I'm not afraid of your brother."

She laughed. "Jason is helping in the church. He told me to take my time and let him know when I'm ready to go. He also said to tell you there's a community picnic here tomorrow."

"Yeah, I think I knew that. And thanks for scaring ten years off my life."

"You aren't afraid. Remember?"

He snaked an arm around her waist. "Not at all."

Beth reached for the door. Game over. "Yeah, neither am I."

"Chicken?" He whispered close to her ear.

"Not at all." She stood on tiptoes and kissed him, pushing the limits because he whispered her name into the kiss and backed away.

She walked down the steps of the RV and across the parking lot calling herself every kind of fool. She was playing with fire. She was playing with her heart and his. Why? To prove she wasn't afraid? To prove to herself that a man could find her attractive, maybe even love her?

Or because she liked the man in question? Maybe she more than liked him. When she'd been fourteen and running barrels she and her friends would twist apple stems to find out the first name of the man they'd marry. One twist for every letter of the alphabet. She'd always made the stem of her apple twist off at the letter J.

Rather than finding Jason she walked to the back

of the church, to an old tree that still shaded the lawn. She'd played here as a kid, under this tree. She'd had plastic horses and cowboys. Her gaze drifted back to the RV. Jeremy had played with her.

And she'd had faith. She'd had a mom who taught her to believe and to pray. Her mom had been so strong—a fighter who battled cancer until she couldn't fight another battle.

At the end she'd turned to this church because she wanted her last weeks to be peaceful, spent with her community and her family. She'd attended church with her head wrapped in scarves and her body frail. Jason and Beth had been at her side. And their father had stayed at home, angry with God.

His anger had spilled over on this church. Today she'd watched him look at the building, his eyes still sad. He connected this church with the wife he lost.

This church. She shaded her eyes with her hand, blocking the bright, afternoon sunlight. This church, faded and worn, had sheltered them. It had provided stories of faith, people who loved one another, songs about Jesus.

Jeremy on one side, the church on the other. Beth rubbed a hand across teary eyes. She wanted to save this church for the memories that were made here and for her mother who had held on to faith here.

And she wanted to back away from the battle for Jeremy.

The answers were no longer simply black and white.

Cancer had taken Beth's mother. Alcohol and bad choices had stolen Jeremy's childhood. This church had been there for all of them. And how long had it taken her to see that? She had wanted to preserve it for her mother's memory, but it was faith she needed to hold on to.

Jason walked around the side of the building. He must have seen her walk this way, or had looked out the window and saw her standing beneath the tree. She smiled at her brother and met him halfway.

"Ready to go?" Jason pushed his hat back and lifted it before settling it into place again.

"Yeah, I'm ready. Is there anything else to do here?"

"No, they have it covered. Jeremy has brought in partitions so the families who are left have their own little areas inside the sanctuary. Did you know that?"

No, she hadn't, but she wasn't surprised. He had watched those people sign her petition and he was still taking care of their needs while they were living in the church.

The church was quiet. Several of the families had moved out. The few that remained were working on the homes they wanted to move back into.

Jeremy walked down the steps of his RV and looked at the big building with the faded paint and the tall steeple. Years ago an old van had picked him up each Sunday, driven by Teddy Buckley. As he got older, Jeremy made sure his little sister was up and ready. Even if they couldn't find her shoes, he took her to church.

Church meant breakfast and sometimes lunch. Church meant a break from his mother passed out on the couch. Or her crazy manic moods when she cleaned and cooked, as if everything was right in their world. He'd never taken a drink in his life, because he wouldn't take the chance of becoming his mother.

He'd always had a plan to get away from her. It was his one real skill set. He was good at sticking to his plans. He had planned a world championship in bull riding and he'd made it. It had taken ten years, but he'd done it. He also had a world title in roping.

He'd planned to build a motorcycle dealership that thrived. He'd done more than that. He'd built a custom bike shop that was doing better than he'd ever dreamed. He wasn't Midas, but he'd done okay for himself. And for his family. He'd helped Elise and her husband. He'd taken care of his mother.

He was still taking care of her.

It was hard to fathom, loving her, even after all she'd done to them. He shook his head and turned away from the church. In the field across the road, cattle were starting to sound the dinner cry. A horse whinnied. He breathed in deep, enjoying the clean smell, the familiar scents. Man, this was home.

He had tried not to let that be his thoughts about this place, but as hard as he tried to push it back, it kept on coming back. This was home. Tulsa was a big house that impressed people. It was traffic, business, playing the right games.

It wasn't home.

He walked across the road to the barn, to the corrals and fences. Pain throbbed lightly in his leg, reminding him of the crazy things he'd done to earn money to buy this place. A dozen years fighting it out on the back of bulls in arenas packed with fans.

It would be a lie to say he hadn't loved that life. He'd loved the traveling. He'd loved the fans. He'd loved the money.

He walked into the big old barn that had been on

this land for more years than he could remember. He'd done some repairs, but the place was still in good shape. Better shape than the house he'd been trying to build. It wasn't good for much more than kindling, thanks to the tornado.

A truck slowed and turned into the driveway of the barn. Jeremy groaned. Too late to pretend he wasn't here. Too late to head out the back door. He guessed it would have to happen sooner or later. He leaned against the side of the barn and waited.

He tried to look casual, arms crossed and hat tipped low. He guessed he probably looked more like an Old West gunslinger than a guy trying to pretend he just didn't care.

"Saw you out here, thought I might stop and see how you're doing." Tim Cooper, otherwise known as his dad, walked up to the barn. He wasn't the young father of a dozen kids anymore. His hair had grayed. The lines in his face were deeper.

Jeremy looked for a reflection of himself in that craggy, suntanned face. Maybe in the light brown hair or the shape of his mouth. Man, maybe it was his walk and the way he managed to look like he really didn't care. But he did.

Or at least Jeremy did.

"I'm doing okay." Jeremy turned to look inside the barn. "I just came out to feed."

"Right. I can help. Or if you need help getting that house frame back up, we can help."

"I can do it."

Tim nodded and took a few steps closer. "I have twelve kids. No, make that thirteen…"

"Are you sure there aren't a few more out there?"

The low blow didn't feel as good as Jeremy thought it might. If he'd been Tim Cooper, he probably would have punched him right then and there.

Tim just rubbed his jaw with his thumb and then he smiled. "I guess I had that coming. But yeah, I'm sure there are no more out there. I messed up, Jeremy. There's no excuse for what I did. I'm not going to blame it on anything other than pure stupidity. When I met up with your mom in Grove, I should have went on home. I didn't. I'm not going to blame it on her, either."

"Then no one is to blame?"

"That isn't what I'm saying. I'm to blame. I hurt a lot of people. I hurt myself, my wife, my kids. That includes you. I should have realized."

"I'm not sure what that means." Jeremy's heart was beating a little faster, a little harder. He walked into the barn, away from a man he wanted to hurt.

"Jeremy, it means you were my son. If your mother would have told me the truth, I would have been there for you."

Jeremy jerked the feed door open. He was thirty years old. He had been kicked, stepped on and head-butted by some of the baddest bulls in the country. He'd never felt this way. He'd never thought he would be this old and still want this man to be his dad. Tim Cooper was a man who admitted his mistakes and tried to do right. Yeah, even Jeremy could see that.

He pulled a bag of feed out and hefted it over his shoulder before glancing back at Tim Cooper. "I guess you'll have to give me the whole story because the only one I have is the one I witnessed and that was my mom screeching in church that you were my dad and you looking pretty stinking embarrassed."

Tim turned a little red. "Yeah, that was a bad day all around."

"I guess that's an understatement." Jeremy walked out the back door of the barn and pushed through the half dozen head of cattle milling around. He pulled a pocketknife out of his pocket and slit the top of the feed bag.

"When I saw that your mother was pregnant, I approached her and asked if you were mine."

"And she didn't tell you the truth."

"She told me there was no way I was your dad."

Jeremy poured the feed into the trough. "That let you off the hook, didn't it? You didn't have to tell your wife. You didn't have to help raise me."

"I would have." Tim stood a short distance away, his gaze shifting from Jeremy to the church. "I should have. I guess I knew. I watched you grow up and I knew. And that was my biggest mistake."

Jeremy shouldered past Tim Cooper. "Yeah, well, it's a little too late now, isn't it?"

"I know that's how you feel."

"Right, you know." Jeremy walked back into the barn. A horse had walked through a stall door and stood in one of the empty stalls. It stuck its nose out at him and he rubbed the animal's face.

"I can't undo the past." Tim Cooper grabbed a flake of hay from the bale in a wheelbarrow.

"None of us can." Jeremy settled into the fact that he was a lot calmer than he thought he'd be. He'd thought about this moment and it had always included his fist connecting with Tim Cooper's smug face.

But Tim Cooper wasn't smug.

And the mad had all drained out of Jeremy.

"I guess Elise isn't yours?" Jeremy turned a five-gallon bucket and sat down. Tim did the same, grabbing an empty bucket and turning it next to Jeremy's.

"No, she isn't." Tim stretched his legs in front of him. "I didn't make a habit of cheating on my wife. I love Angie. I hurt her and I've had to live with that."

"She's a good woman." He absently rubbed his leg and he didn't look at Tim. "If you're doing this because you think it'll make me change my mind about the church, you're wrong. I do think it is pretty sad that you all neglected it all these years and now you suddenly care."

Tim sighed. "We didn't neglect it. We accepted that our community was changing. Years ago, people stayed in Dawson. They farmed. They raised their kids here. They went to church here. That meant every church in town was full. Life changed, people moved or they wanted bigger churches. It's hard to get a pastor to come to a church like Back Street in a town the size of Dawson. It isn't as if we had a lot to pay."

"Yeah, I guess I can see that." Jeremy glanced to the left, across the street to the church.

"That church didn't hurt you. I did."

"You're right about that." Jeremy pushed himself up from the bucket and wished he hadn't sat on something so low to the ground. He grimaced and flexed his leg. He figured it was probably going to rain pretty soon. For the sake of those recovering from the tornado, he hoped it didn't.

"Jeremy, I'd like for us to spend some time together."

"Let's not push it, Tim. It wasn't that long ago that you tried to buy me off."

"You misunderstood. I was trying to make up for what I did, not…"

"Yeah, we have a different memory on that."

"I hope you'll give me a chance. We're having a birthday party for Heather. Maybe you could join us."

Heather Cooper was one of the nicest girls Jeremy knew. He had defended her once, in high school. Now he realized he'd been defending his little sister. He should have known.

It took him a minute to process thoughts that hadn't sunk in before. When he'd been busy being mad he hadn't thought about how this connected him to people he'd always known. Yeah, Jackson had been in his face, but that was Jackson.

Heather Cooper was his little sister. The man standing in front of him was his dad. It took time for all that to sink in. He'd spent the last dozen years running from it instead of working through it.

"I'll think about it."

"Bring a date if you want." Tim waved and walked out of the barn. "The party starts in two hours."

Right, bring a date. The whole "welcome to the family" wagon might be pushing things. It wasn't that easy, to just move on and suddenly be a Cooper. But Jeremy was willing to give it a try.

Chapter Ten

The box was open on Beth's bed. It shouldn't make her feel this way, as if her mother had just left. Opening the box was like opening up the past, the forgotten pain. Beth brushed at her eyes and sat down on the bed. Why had her dad waited so long? Had he been afraid she couldn't handle the memories? Or had he been unable to handle seeing her with these things of her mother's?

She lifted the ring box from among the contents and lifted the lid. Emotion clogged her throat and tears burned her eyes. Her mother's wedding ring. The diamond glinted in the overhead light, sparkling in the gold setting.

Beth slid the ring on her finger, the one where she'd worn Chance's ring for eight years. She'd hocked the ring the day she left him because she'd needed money to run, to hide. Now she smiled, because it was ironic that the ring was the one good thing he'd done for her in their marriage.

She picked up the journal that had been hidden in the box all these years. It was yellowed with age and smelled a little musty. But it was her mother's story.

Five years of battling cancer and having faith. Beth felt a healthy dose of shame. Her mother had never lost faith. Beth had. A few battles and she'd jumped ship and tried to manage life on her own.

It hadn't worked out so well.

Things were getting better, though. Her faith was getting stronger.

She opened the journal to one of her mother's shorter notes, a day when she'd felt defeated. And she'd ended the short entry by quoting Psalm 91. *He who dwelleth in the secret place of the most high, shall abide in the shadow of the almighty. And I will say of the Lord, He is my refuge and my fortress. My God. In Him will I trust.*

In Him will I trust.

Beth put the journal on her nightstand and placed the lid on the box. A light knock on her door, tentative and cautious. She wiped at her eyes and took a deep breath.

"Come in."

The door eased open. Her dad peeked in. "I have that new gelding down at the stable. Do you want to try him out?"

His gaze slid to the box and to the journal. He inhaled sharply and glanced away.

"Dad, she would have wanted you to move on, to…"

"No." He shook his head, gray hair thinning and weathered lines creasing his face. "Beth, we all deal with things in a different way. I've dealt with this nearly your entire life."

"I know." Because they'd found the cancer soon after Beth's birth. Had he ever blamed her?

"How's Lorna?"

Her dad didn't smile. And then he did. "I guess she's doing fine. Come on down and see if you think this gelding will suit you."

"I'll be down in a few minutes."

She picked up the note she'd gotten from the historical society that day. They hadn't found a real reason to register Back Street Church as an historical building. She folded the piece of paper and shoved it into the pocket of her jeans.

When she got to the barn the horse was already saddled. It was a good-looking roan, brown and sprinkled with gray and hints of chestnut. The horse turned, ears twitching at Beth's arrival.

Beth's dad walked out of an empty stall. She smiled because his step was lighter these days. She'd come home. He said that had made things a lot easier for him. But Lorna was the one responsible for the lighter step, the easier smile.

"Want to try him in the arena?" Her dad unclipped the lead rope from the hook on the wall.

"Sure." She took the reins and led the horse out the door and to the arena. The white boards of the arena needed painting. She'd have her dad pick up the paint and she'd do that next week, when things settled down a little.

Her dad opened the gate to the arena and she led the gelding through. He side-stepped a little and she pulled him close, brushing a hand down his neck. Probably a good idea to lunge him a bit before riding him, but she hadn't brought a rope out with her. She glanced back, sometimes there was a long line wrapped and hanging on the corner post. Not this time.

She led him once around the arena instead and then she slipped her foot into the stirrup and swung her right leg over the horse's back. As she settled into the saddle a truck pulled up the drive. She reined the horse around and watched Jeremy get out of the big Ford. He was dressed in a polo and jeans. He'd left his hat at home. Did that mean he was going out, or was he leaving? Did he know about the historical society decision?

He was a little overdressed for a neighborly visit.

No sense dwelling on what might happen. Or might not. She loosened the reins and nudged the horse forward. The gelding broke into an easy trot. She moved her hand and gave him another light nudge with her heels. He moved into an easy lope around the arena. She neck reined him to the left, leaning the reins lightly against the right side of his neck. He took the lead and circled in a tight circle. Nice.

She tightened her legs and he slowed to a walk, just the lightest pressure on the reins. Her dream horse. She smiled as she rode back to her dad. He was standing next to Jeremy.

"Dad, he's great."

"He's off a little," Jeremy answered. He opened the gate and walked in.

"No, he isn't." She eased the horse back and he tucked his head against the pressure and backed up. She released and he stepped forward and stopped.

"Yeah, he is." Her dad rested his arms on the top of the gate. "Right leg, Jeremy."

"Yes, sir." Jeremy ran his hand down the horse's neck. He touched the horse's rear leg and eased his hand down. "Pretty warm, Beth."

"Well, that's just wrong." She slid off the horse and

walked around to the side where Jeremy was lifting the horse's rear leg. The gelding pulled a little but Jeremy leaned into his side and held the leg up.

"He might have pulled a tendon in the ride up from Oklahoma City. Or maybe he hit it against the trailer." Her dad walked through the gate and closed it behind him.

"It's a little swollen." Jeremy released the leg. "Doesn't look like anything serious, but I'd call Joe."

"Yeah, I will." Her dad shook his head. "He's a nice animal."

"I'll take him in and put him in a stall." Beth took the reins from Jeremy. "What are you all dressed up for?"

Jeremy looked down, as if he hadn't noticed the jeans, or the unscuffed boots he was dragging through the dusty arena.

"I'm on my way to Heather's birthday party."

He said it like he went to birthday parties at the Coopers' every day of the week. But Beth wondered. She glanced back as she walked toward the gate with the gelding. He smiled, a tight smile, a little tense.

"It'll be fun." She led the gelding through the gate. The men followed.

"Let me take him. We'll wrap that leg up and call the vet." Her dad took the reins.

"Would you like to go with me?" Jeremy rubbed the back of his neck and shifted a nervous look at Buck. Jeremy was thirty and afraid of her dad.

"Sounds like a good idea." Her dad stopped and the horse stopped next to him. The big roan hung his head, looking for all the world as if he thought he'd let them down. Beth ran a hand over the horse's soft, sleek neck.

"Go with you to the Coopers'? I don't know, that might be a little awkward."

"Tim said to bring a date."

Beth smiled then. "A date, huh?"

"Well, yeah."

A date. She looked down at her own faded jeans and the T-shirt she'd put on earlier, after cleaning house. "I would have to get ready."

Jeremy glanced at his watch. "We don't have to be there for thirty minutes. I'll unsaddle the horse and help your dad get him settled."

"I'll hurry."

Jeremy held the gelding while Beth's dad wrapped the animal's leg. He'd already called the vet and so now it was down to putting the horse in a stall and waiting.

"She's been through a lot."

Jeremy had been stroking the gray flecked neck of the horse and he looked down, meeting the serious gaze of Buck Bradshaw.

"Yes, sir, I know she has."

This had to be one of those conversations when the father was asking about intentions toward his daughter. Jeremy didn't have an answer. He couldn't tell Buck that he'd come here with a definite plan, part revenge and part business. He'd known day by day what to do and how to go about doing it. But now, his life was minute by minute and things just kept changing.

Beth was one of the unknowns in his plan. He remembered something in science about unknown properties. Yeah, Beth had definitely changed the equation and he had a feeling she might change the outcome.

Buck Bradshaw stood and patted the horse on the

rump. He was a big guy, burly. Maybe he was getting older, but he was still solid. He could probably still hurt a guy.

"So?" Buck pushed his hat back and looked Jeremy square in the face.

"I'm thinking she's a wonderful person and I'm glad she's a friend."

Buck's chin dropped and inch and he stared. "She went through a lot with Chance."

"I know she did."

Jeremy wanted to remind Buck that Chance was back in town, staying at his parents' place. He was being investigated for damage to Beth's truck. Jeremy wasn't going to hurt Beth. And he'd sure make sure no one else did.

But he didn't know what that meant about his plans.

"Keep her safe." Buck stepped out of the stall and closed the door.

"I intend on doing just that." Jeremy walked out of the barn with Buck. The sun was low on the horizon and a few hazy clouds turned the sky pink and lavender.

Beth walked across the yard, her dark hair loose. She had changed into jeans that were rolled up above her ankles, and a button-down shirt. The boots she'd worn had been replaced by glitzy little sandals. Gloss shimmered on her lips, drawing his gaze when she smiled.

"Ready?" He cleared his throat and tried again. "Ready to go?"

"I'm ready. I hope this isn't a dressy event."

"It's taking place in Tim and Angie's backyard."

"Right." She looked down and shrugged.

"Beth, you look fine." He wanted to comment about

the distressed jeans with the tiny holes above the knees and the bright red of her toenails.

He nodded a quick goodbye to her father and led her to his truck. He didn't hold her hand. She didn't reach for his. He opened the door and she climbed in, smiling as she clicked her seat belt in place and he closed the door.

It was a five-minute drive to the Coopers'. He'd never been one to get too worked up, but this case of nerves rolled around inside him. Beth glanced his way and smiled. He was focused on the road when her hand touched his arm.

"They're the same people you've known all your life." Her words were spoken softly as they turned up the driveway that led to the big Georgian-style home.

"Right. But growing up they were the family I always wished I'd had."

They were the family he hadn't had. It made bitter a real easy pill to swallow.

"I guess we have to let go of the past and all of the regret, the things we wish we'd had or wish we'd done differently."

He smiled at Beth and after shifting he reached for her tiny hand. It slid into his, fingers interlaced. She knew about regret. She knew about loss.

"Thanks for coming with me."

"Because you couldn't have done it without me?" She smiled and gave his hand a light squeeze before letting go and slipping her hand from his.

"I think that's probably what I would have said."

He parked and stepped out of the truck. Beth was out before he could reach her side. They walked up to the house together, her fingers brushing his as they walked side by side. He didn't reach for her hand. That would have connected them and they didn't need connections right now.

The front door opened as they walked up the steps. Angie Cooper wore an apron over her jeans and T-shirt. She smiled and waved them inside.

"I'm so glad you're here." She hugged Jeremy and then Beth. "Tim is manning the grill out back. I hope you're hungry."

"Starving," Beth said.

She eased her hand into his and smiled up at him, in a way that set him on his heels because it reached deep inside and forced him to be someone different, someone a lot stronger than he'd ever been before. Maybe someone a lot more forgiving.

He stopped in the two-story entryway. Angie had continued down the hall expecting them to follow her, probably to the kitchen and out to the patio. Jeremy rubbed the back of his neck where tension had settled in the muscles.

"Jeremy?" Beth slid a finger through his belt loop and pulled him close. "Relax. This is your family."

"You two coming?" Angie had reappeared. She stood in the hall and beckoned for them to follow.

Jeremy took a deep breath. "Yeah, we're coming."

Beth exhaled, as if she hadn't been sure. That made two of them.

The patio ran the entire length of the house. A covered outdoor kitchen at the far end, complete with a grill, sink and fire pit, seemed to be the popular meeting place. Jeremy glanced around, noticing that the visitors were all family. Of course with the Cooper clan, that meant a couple of dozen people, give or take.

Reese, Jackson, Travis, Jesse, even Blake was there. They were sitting around the pool, iced tea in hand. Maggie Cooper Jones was trying to corral her three kids. Lucky was sitting with his wife. Their daughter was in her early teens and she'd just dived into the pool.

Heather was at a patio table with Mia. There were a couple of kids missing.

He was a member of this family. As a kid he would have jumped in without thinking. Today he stood back and watched because as an adult he questioned how they felt about him being there, in the middle of their family. If it had been him, he might have been a little angry.

But they were all long past being teenagers. They'd been dealing with this for the last twelve years, same as him. They just hadn't dealt with it together. That's where Jeremy had made the choice, one he couldn't undo.

Jackson nodded in his direction and stood up. That started a migration.

"Everyone, look who's joining us, Jeremy and Beth." Angie touched his arm and smiled.

She knew how to take in kids, even the grown and angry kind. He had his past, she'd had her own to deal with. She'd had to deal with finding out about him. That made her one of the strongest women he knew.

The Coopers didn't give him long to think about his past or what Angie had been through. They didn't give him a chance to worry about his reception. As he stood there getting his bearings, the Cooper family stampeded. The girls, his half sister and adopted sisters gave him hugs and they cried.

His brothers slapped him on the back and gave him

fisted man-hugs. Tim manned the grill and smiled at his wife and then at Jeremy.

This was the closest thing he'd ever had to a family, a real family. He'd had his church family when he was a kid. He'd had the guys he traveled with when he rode bulls. He'd taken care of his mom and his sister.

"Want a glass of iced tea?" Heather smiled and led him to the stainless steel fridge under the counter that connected to the grill. "Sorry, we can be overwhelming."

"A little."

"I'm sorry, you know, that we didn't get to grow up together." And then she shrugged. "But in a way, I guess we did. Back Street kept us all connected."

"Heather, let's not talk about the church. Not tonight."

She looked startled and then she nodded. "I didn't say that as a prelude to a 'please don't tear it down' conversation."

"You'll have to forgive me if I say that it sounds like a few of the other conversations I've had lately."

"It probably does and I'm sorry. Let's forget it and join the party. Beth is talking to Jackson."

That stirred an emotion a little different than the one he'd just battled, and a lot more confusing.

Tim caught him before he could make it to Beth's side. He flipped steaks on the grill and offered Jeremy a bottle of water.

"I'm good."

"I'm glad you came."

Jeremy looked around, at this family, his family. "Yeah, so am I."

He'd let the last twelve years of running keep him

from being here with them. That was just about the craziest thing he'd ever done. Because in the last week they'd proven over and over again that it might have been nice to have them all involved in his life.

Even if Jackson was on the big side of being a pain. And at that moment he was leading Beth over to the flower gardens.

Tim slapped him on the back and laughed. "You might want to hold on to her. I think Jackson is starting to think about settling down."

"She's a free woman." Jeremy's words sounded tight to his own hearing.

"Yes, she is. She's thrown you a curveball on this church situation."

"That she has."

"I hope you don't let that come between the two of you."

Jeremy shrugged it off because it was better if something did come between them. Might as well be the church.

Tim shook seasoning on the steaks. "These are nearly done. You know, if this becomes a legal battle for you, it might be cheaper to let it go and build elsewhere."

Yeah, that made sense. But he hated to back down from a fight.

Beth knew that Jackson was messing with Jeremy, even before he whispered that his brother's brown eyes were starting to turn kind of green. He shouldered against her and laughed. She laughed, because Jackson had always been the flirt, but never the guy she was interested in dating.

"I should go sit with him." She shot a look in Jeremy's

direction. He'd taken a seat next to Reese and was pretending to drink water and not glare. She reached into her pocket where she'd stuck the note before leaving the house.

She could at least give him this. It might make him frown less.

"If he hurts you, I'll take care of him." Jackson walked with her, away from the flower gardens that Angie Cooper tended herself.

"He isn't going to hurt me."

Jackson shrugged. "He's never been much of a settling-down kind of guy."

"A little like his older brother?"

Jackson laughed at that. "I guess you got me there. But if the right woman came along, I might just give up my single ways."

"It happens that way, Jackson."

"Yeah, it does."

They were at the table where Reese and Jackson were discussing the army and Reese leaving for basic training. Jeremy pushed out the chair next to him. Reese made some kind of crazy excuse why he had to leave.

"Nothing like matchmaking, is there?" Jeremy leaned close to her and she loved that he smelled like the outdoors and clean soap.

"It isn't my favorite thing in the world." She pulled the note out of her pocket. Keep it to herself or show it to him?

"What's that?" Jeremy reached and she handed him the note about the historical society's ruling.

"You win this battle." She met his caramel gaze and held it, wanting him to smile. "They voted against the church becoming a historical site."

He read the note and he didn't smile. "I don't want this to be a battle. I never wanted that."

"I made it a battle, didn't I?"

He smiled then and leaned to kiss her cheek. "You did. And I'm afraid there won't be any winners."

No, there wouldn't be winners. She thought about telling him he could walk away, but what if he did? What if he gave up and left?

Chapter Eleven

Back Street Church on Sunday morning was full to capacity with members of Dawson Community Church and various other residents of Dawson. A few came out of curiosity, others were there to say "thank you" to God for sparing them, others were steadfast members of the community church who needed a place to go on Sunday morning until their church was repaired.

Speaking of repairs, Beth stood in the yard and looked up at the church. Some repairs had taken place at Back Street. The people using it as a shelter had helped. And so had Jeremy. She'd seen him on a ladder that morning, repairing loose gutters on the roof over the porch.

A door closed. She glanced to her right and watched him walk down the steps of the RV, a little less gimpy than a few days ago. Last night after Heather's birthday party he'd driven her home. He'd walked her to the door. He hadn't kissed her good-night. As a matter of fact, he hadn't said much after she'd shown him the note. And she was kind of sorry she'd given it to him if that's how he was going to act.

Like a sore winner.

She glanced his way again. He smiled and nodded. She walked up the steps, greeted Wyatt Johnson at the door and walked into the building.

It no longer smelled like dust and age. The inside had been polished and cleaned. The windows had been washed and sunlight lit up the old stained glass. The sanctuary glowed with warm light and the warmth of a hundred people. Beth stopped in the vestibule and took a deep breath. This was how it felt to come home.

She'd been attending Dawson Community Church for several months, but this church was home. Today it looked like it had years ago. It wasn't shadowy and empty, draped with spiderwebs.

Her heart wasn't empty. Faith had been returning, seeping in through the cracks in her heart.

God wasn't a bitter father pushing her from what was familiar and comforting. He wasn't an angry husband, using his word to beat her into submission.

He was God the father, compassionate, merciful and offering grace to a broken life. Her life.

"We'll walk in together."

Her dad stood next to her, surprising her. There were two people she didn't expect to see in this service. He was definitely one of them. And next to him, Lorna. A public acknowledgement of their relationship.

"I haven't been in here in years." Buck Bradshaw shook his head. "Your mom and I were kids in this church, and then we were teens. And then I got busy with the farm and she kept coming. I guess that happens."

"It can." Beth reached for his hand, rough and strong. He'd always been strong. They walked down the aisle together. Beth stopped at the second pew from the front, the pew where she'd always sat with her mother and brother. The third pew was where Jeremy sat with their Sunday school teacher.

Her dad didn't move. He held tight to her hand and looked at the carpet runner that covered the center aisle. Dark brown, faded and worn. Someone had found it in a closet and unrolled it.

"I didn't want to lose her. I wanted God to heal her." He looked up, his brown eyes watery.

"Dad, we don't have to do this." Beth let go of his hand and sat down. She slid down the pew and made room for her father and for Lorna. It pulled at her heart a little, to see Lorna next to her father.

After so many years it should have been easier. But it felt as if they had all gotten stuck in time, not moving forward, because they had avoided church, and sometimes they'd avoided one another. They had avoided honest discussion.

Her dad sighed as he took his seat.

"No, we don't have to," Buck's voice rasped. "But we should have done this a long time ago. I should have told you how much I loved her and didn't want to lose her. I should have told you how much I prayed."

Beth leaned against him, shoulder to shoulder. "Dad, it's okay."

He shook his head, "I let her down. I told her I would hold us together."

"We did the best we could. How were you supposed to know how much it would hurt?"

"No, I guess no one ever knows." A tear trickled down his cheek.

Wyatt Johnson took the place behind the pulpit. He smiled at the crowd and shook his head.

"Disaster has a way of bringing us all together. The important thing is to keep that unity after the healing is done."

The rest of the sermon was lost because Beth looked back and saw Jeremy enter the church. He removed his hat and stood at the back of the building. Her heart beat in double time and her eyes overflowed.

Her dad pushed a box of tissues into her hands. "Might need those."

She sniffled and nodded. She had failed to change Jeremy's mind. Maybe God could do what she couldn't. Back Street Church still had a purpose. She hoped she wasn't the only one who saw the need.

Jeremy left before the service ended. He made eye contact with Wyatt, slipped his hat back on his head and walked out. The sunlight was bright. The sky was bluer than blue. He stood on the front porch of the church and stared out at the field that he'd baled the day before. The big, round bales dotted the pasture. His cattle grazed among the bales.

His cattle. His land. His church. That last part didn't feel as good as the rest. What had started as a simple plan now knotted inside his gut like the worst idea he'd ever had. Maybe he'd always known he wouldn't be able to do it.

The dozer was still sitting on the trailer.

So what did he do now? Head back to Tulsa? He glanced back into the church and his gaze attached to the back of Beth's dark head. She turned and smiled, as if she'd known he was there, watching her.

Last night had changed things and he still didn't know how. He didn't know if he'd given up on the church or if he'd given up on being here because he didn't know how to be a Cooper, a citizen of Dawson or a man in Beth's life. He didn't even know why that last part was in the equation.

If he went back to Tulsa, he could slip back into his old life. He kind of liked that life. It was definitely a lot less complicated. He could keep this land, build his shop and let someone else manage the place. That had been his initial plan. He'd never considered living here full time. He'd planned on building a house where he could stay once in a while.

He was Jeremy Hightree, not Jeremy Cooper. He could climb on the back of a bull and never break a sweat, never get lost in fear or the battle for the championship. Cool on the back of a bull, that was what they'd said about him.

Yesterday he'd bought a basketball net. Actually, he'd bought two. He shook his head as he walked across the parking lot to his RV. Impulse shopping. He'd also bought a cheap volleyball set. He'd been planning activities for the community picnic that they were holding today on the grounds of Back Street Church.

He was starting to see that he was in a real crisis. He looked up and shook his head. He'd always heard that a guy couldn't outrun God.

Well, a guy could sure try.

But today he was going to finish putting together a basketball net, because the kids deserved something to do. He pulled his toolbox out of the back of his truck and grabbed one of the folding chairs from in front of his RV.

When the church bell rang, signaling the end of the service, the basketball net was finished. He lifted it and went for the sand that he'd use to fill the base. A truck drove by. He didn't recognize it. But he recognized the man behind the wheel and seeing him set Jeremy's blood to boiling. Chance Martin. Obviously he hadn't gotten the message about staying away from Beth.

Jeremy stopped walking and watched the other man slow down and glance in the direction of the church. It would be a cold day in a hot place before Jeremy would let that man lay one hand on Beth.

People were streaming out of the building and down the steps. Jeremy watched for Beth. He glanced back, saw that Chance had stopped his truck.

Where was Beth? And why in the world would Chance choose today, in front of this crowd, to cause problems?

Maybe he wouldn't. Jeremy liked the thought that the other man would pull on down the road and leave well enough alone. It was Sunday. Jeremy didn't want to have to hurt this guy, not today, not on Sunday.

Beth walked out the front door of the church, talking to Rachel Johnson, Wyatt's wife. The two were laughing, totally oblivious to Chance's presence. Jeremy put the sandbag he carried on the base of the basketball net and started toward Beth.

A truck door slammed. He glanced toward the road and saw Chance heading across the lawn of the church, pushing through the crowd. Jeremy picked up his pace. He reached the steps of the church right after Chance. Jeremy wasn't alone. More than a dozen men had noticed the situation. Including Jason Bradshaw who was fast-tracking toward his sister.

Beth stood on the porch, her eyes large, focused on Chance.

"Chance, I think you should leave." Jeremy took a step forward, putting himself on the steps of the church.

"Jeremy, I'd recommend you stay back from my wife." Chance turned to face him. He'd been a skinny kid back in school. He'd outgrown that phase.

"I'm not your wife, Chance." Beth walked down the steps. Jeremy wanted to stop her, but man, she looked determined. She looked like a woman who wasn't backing down. Maybe she'd done too much of that in the past.

"Yes, Beth, you're my wife. We were married legal and binding and that divorce document doesn't mean a thing to me."

"I'm not afraid anymore, Chance. I'm not going to let you quote verses to scare me. I'm not going to let you use God as an excuse for hurting me. I'm not afraid."

Jeremy wanted to cheer her on, but he could only stand there and wait. She was beautiful and strong, but he could see her legs trembling. She sneaked a glance in his direction and he smiled.

And then Chance rushed up the steps and grabbed her. Taken by surprise, Jeremy was a stupid moment too late. He watched as Chance's hand came up, connecting with Beth's face. And then he took the steps two at a time and made it just in time to grab Chance Martin as he fell backward, groaning in pain.

Jeremy held Chance by the arms. The other man was fighting mad and Beth stood there trembling but okay, rubbing the fist that had punched Chance. A bruise was already turning her cheek blue. That bruise went all over Jeremy. He pulled his hand back and spun Chance around. A hand grabbed his fist.

"Bad idea." Jackson shook his head and grinned. "There's a deputy pulling up. Why don't you let me take Chance to meet his destiny?"

Jackson grabbed Chance and Jeremy watched them walk away. He took a deep shaky breath and turned to find Beth still standing on the steps of the church. Jason had a protective arm around her and Buck had turned and was headed in the direction of the patrol car.

"You okay?"

"I'm good." Her chin came up a notch. He recognized someone trying to be strong. He'd made that same move too many times to count. It had started when he was a kid and some well-meaning grown-up would ask if he needed anything.

He was always good.

Even when he was a kid and scared to death.

"Yeah, I know you are." He didn't reach for her hand. Instead he changed the subject. "Want to see what I've been doing while you were in church?"

The cop was putting Chance in the back of the patrol car.

She smiled a wavering smile. "You were in there, too."

"Yeah, I was there, too."

Jason moved, let his sister go. "Take a walk, sis. This will blow over and everyone will calm down."

She nodded and joined Jeremy. He didn't reach for her hand, didn't put his arm around her. Instead they headed for his RV and the parking lot, not touching but walking side-by-side.

They didn't make it far. The deputy caught up with

them, tall and purposeful, his hand on his sidearm, probably out of habit. Domestic abuse ranked as one of the most dangerous calls a cop could make.

Beth hugged herself and watched the officer approach. How many times had she lived through similar moments? She weaved a little. So much for being strong. He wrapped an arm around her waist and held her close.

"Beth, do you want to press charges?" Officer Hall stopped in front of them. He was an older deputy. Jeremy remembered him from years ago. He'd been to their house more than once. A few times, along with caseworkers from family services.

"I..." Beth glanced at the patrol car. How many times in the past had she said no? "Yes. I do want to press charges."

"It's what you need to do, Beth." Jason Bradshaw joined them. He smiled at his sister. "You aren't alone anymore. He doesn't have a right to hit you."

"I know." Finally she nodded. "I want to press charges."

Jeremy stepped away and he watched Beth talking to the officer. He watched her fill out a form on the clipboard she'd been handed. Once she glanced his way. Did she want him to stand next to her, to be there with her as she did the one thing she'd always feared doing?

He pulled his keys out of his pocket and walked to his truck. All around him the good folks of Dawson were having fun. They were having a picnic on the grounds of Back Street Church. The kids were already shooting hoops and someone had set up the volleyball net. It leaned precariously to the east and the girls playing were laughing and having a great time with the cheap ball and net.

He suddenly flashed back twenty years, when he was a kid of ten, tossing a ball to one of the Cooper boys while Tim talked to the pastor. Jeremy shook free from the memory and climbed into his truck.

Beth finished filling out the complaint against Chance. She glanced in the back of the patrol car. His head was down. He looked contrite. In a moment he would smile at her. He would mouth an apology and ask her to forgive him. She knew because this was a scene that had played out too often in their marriage.

"Beth, don't let him make you feel sorry." Jason was at her side. She smiled up at him.

"Not this time." She looked away from the car, back to the church and to the people she'd known all of her life. "No, I'm not going to feel guilty for what he did."

She'd done that too many times in the past. She'd changed her mind, told the officer she wasn't pressing charges. Her husband was sorry. He hadn't meant to hurt her. Now, remembering, her heart shook. She had been the victim but each time the police came, and he had made her feel as if she deserved the abuse. She had deserved the bruises.

In the end, the broken arm.

But she hadn't deserved it. She had been a victim who didn't know how to walk away. She had believed him when he told her the abuse was her fault.

"He has a problem." She was proud of herself for being able to make that statement. She knew it had to be a huge first step in being strong and moving on with her life.

Step two would be convincing herself that someday someone could love her without seeing all of her flaws. Eight years of being told no one else would want her had left scars far deeper than anything he could have put on her body.

She smiled up at her brother. "I'm worth more than that."

Jason's strong arms wrapped around her in a giant brother-hug. "I'm glad to hear you say that."

"Thank you for all the times you tried to convince me to leave."

"I'm your brother, I wanted to do more."

"You gave me the way out."

"I guess I would have done anything to get you back home safe."

She nodded and wiped at her eyes. Their dad was still talking to the deputy. He walked away and joined them, his smile a little fierce. He hugged Beth tight, holding her against him in a choking hug that buried her face against his shoulder.

"Dad. Can't. Breathe."

His laugh was shaky and he let her go. "I'm glad we're all together."

"Me, too." Beth glanced toward the RV and the empty parking space. Jeremy's truck was gone. He was gone.

"He left a few minutes ago." Jason sighed. "Let's get back to this picnic. Our town could use a little bit of a break. So could we."

"Vera brought a dozen pies." Buck Bradshaw had bought the pies. Beth would keep that secret for her dad. He often did little things for people in the community and rarely did anyone find out that he was the person responsible.

When Camp Hope had hit a financial snag last year, her dad had been a factor in keeping the camp going. He said it was a good thing to give kids a place to go in the summer.

It all felt a little empty when she thought about Jeremy leaving the picnic. When she thought about him leaving at all.

"Do you think he feels guilty?"

Jason stopped walking. "Chance?"

"No, Jeremy. Do you think it bothers him to watch people enjoying the church when he's planning to knock it down in a matter of days?"

Jason shrugged. "I don't know. I guess it would bother him. Or maybe he's changed his mind."

"I don't think he has." But last night she'd given him the note and he hadn't been as happy as she would have thought.

An old sedan pulled in the parking lot. Jason raised a hand in greeting. "I'm going to help Etta. She went home for some clothing Alyson's mom sent to help out."

"That's nice of her. How's Alyson feeling?"

"Very pregnant." He grinned. "Want to help me grab this stuff from Etta's car?"

"Sure." But her mind tripped her up. Because she'd always wanted a baby of her own. She had always wanted to be a wife, a mom. But it was easier to help Jason than to think about the future, or about Jeremy walking away. Jeremy shouldn't be in her dreams of forever. But she had a hard time erasing those thoughts.

Chapter Twelve

Jeremy left Tim Cooper's on Monday and drove down the narrow paved road to the trailer he'd grown up in. He'd always known the truth about this place and his upbringing, but seeing it after being at the Cooper ranch made it seem all the smaller, made his childhood a little sketchier.

He walked into the dingy single-wide that had been his home for the first eighteen years of his life and he let out a deep breath, whistling as he looked around. He should have come sooner. He'd just been putting off the inevitable.

Ten feet wide, fifty feet long. Two bedrooms and a bathroom with a floor that sagged. He stood in the tiny living room and tried hard not to go back in time, to sleeping on that old, plaid sofa every night.

He wasn't here for a trip down memory lane, he was here to pack. He'd met with his mother's doctor that morning and the nursing home director. She wouldn't be returning home.

He glanced around the room with the fake wood paneling and carpet from the 1970s. Maybe one of the families that had lost their home could use this place until theirs was repaired. He'd talk to Wyatt.

As much as he didn't want to take a trip back, the trailer did it for him. He walked down the narrow hall, past the room where Elise had slept. It wasn't any bigger than his walk-in closet. It had room for a twin bed and a dresser, but not much else.

It should have been easy to put this behind him. He should cowboy up and let it all go. But it wasn't that easy. He could tough it out on the back of a bull, ride through his injuries, but this place held a lifetime of bad memories.

Too much of the past included how this place treated his sister. A guy could pull on a pair of jeans and a T-shirt and let it all be good. A girl, not so easy.

Elise had cried as they stood at the edge of the yard waiting for the bus. She'd cried because she was cold. She'd cried because her jeans were too short. And too many times she'd cried because she was hungry. It hit him deep, because as a kid he hadn't been able to do anything about it.

His mother had been drunkenly oblivious to his little sister's pain.

He slammed his palm against the wall. The first time didn't do it. The second time helped. The sting bit through the skin of his palm, but it didn't lessen his anger with this past. He walked back down the hall and out the front door.

The porch sagged and a couple of the boards were splintered. The handrail had long since fallen off. Jeremy jerked off his hat and swiped his arm across his face. Man, it was hot for so early in the summer. He walked down the steps to his truck. He had boxes from the convenience store in the back. Not that there was much in this place to pack up.

A truck turned the corner and eased up the road, stopping at his driveway. He shook his head and leaned against the bed of his truck. Beth didn't know how to leave well enough alone.

He grabbed the boxes out of the back of the truck and leaned them against the back tire. Beth pulled in the drive and stopped. She didn't hurry to get out of the truck she'd been driving. One of her dad's old farm trucks. She smiled through the tinted window.

Was she waiting for an invitation?

Yeah, probably. He nodded and she jumped out of the truck. What he didn't get was why in the world did this all get a little easier when she showed up?

"What's up?" She slowed her pace as she got closer, as if she suddenly doubted the decision to stop. Second thoughts. Yeah, that made two of them.

"I need to pack. I guess maybe someone could use a temporary place to stay."

"That would be nice." She glanced at the trailer and back at him. "What about your mom?"

"She won't be coming home."

"I'm sorry."

"Yeah, well, that's the way life is." He picked up the half dozen boxes and walked toward the trailer. Beth followed, her pace a little quicker to keep up with his.

He slowed.

"I'll help you." She followed him up the steps.

Jeremy stopped at the screen door, held it open and turned to look at the woman behind him. The memory of Chance going after her flashed through his mind.

That fresh anger pushed the past to the far recesses of his mind. He couldn't change the past.

No reason to dwell there, either. At this point he sure didn't know what the future held.

Beth took a step back and nearly fell backward when her foot hit one of the broken steps. His hand shot out and he pulled her back up.

"Maybe this wasn't a good idea. I'm not sure what I was thinking."

"Beth, stay."

He touched her cheek, the place where Chance's hand had connected with soft skin. The blue and green of the bruise had spread out across her cheekbone. She flinched when his fingers touched the area.

Something shook loose inside him. He pulled her close and held her tight. When she relaxed against him, he kissed the top of her head, getting lost in her, in the sweetness of her hands on his arms, the soft scent of her, the way her head fit against his chest.

"I would never hurt you." Jeremy whispered the promise and he knew it shouldn't matter so much. How did he keep a promise like that when nearly everything he had planned would hurt her in some way?

She pulled back and looked up at him. "Let's get stuff packed."

With a nod he opened the screen door again. He grabbed the boxes and held the door open for Beth to take that first step into the home where he'd grown up. He hadn't brought anyone here as a kid, not as a teen, not ever. Most kids wouldn't have wanted to come here. Most parents wouldn't have allowed it.

He watched her expression, saw the flicker of emotion in her eyes. He glanced around, seeing what she saw. The living room and kitchen, dirty dishes still in the sink and empty bottles of booze on the counter. The trash overflowed and flies swarmed.

"Where do we start?"

He smiled. Was that all she had to say? He handed her a box. "I guess we pack up all this junk my mom called her 'collectibles.'"

"Do you have tape?" Beth grabbed one of the flattened boxes and pulled it into shape.

"In the truck." He walked to the door. "Thanks for helping."

"Jobs like this are easier with a friend."

He nodded and walked out the door. Man, he'd never needed fresh air so badly in his life. He needed space. He stood in the yard and scanned the field, the neighboring farms. He'd lived here his whole life but he'd never seen it like this, as a place he didn't want to run from.

And inside the trailer, Beth was packing up junk from his past. He needed to get his head on straight and remember his plan. It was getting a little easier with the ruling from the historical society in his favor. In a few days the planning and zoning committee would make a decision on the petition, to zone or not zone the property for commercial use.

Too bad he no longer knew what his plan was. Yeah, the church, the business; but Beth had changed everything, right down to his old resentments that had driven him to bring that dozer to Dawson. Revenge wasn't quite as sweet as he'd once thought it would be, back when it was all about him.

He kind of missed the old Jeremy, the one who knew how to let go and not take relationships too seriously.

Beth was the type of woman a guy married, had babies with, grew old with. She'd already been hurt. She deserved a lot better than a guy with his kind of baggage. That was one thing her dad had been right about. When he'd caught him by the ear that summer at the rodeo ground, he'd told Jeremy that Beth was worth way more than some kid who didn't have squat to his name.

Jeremy wasn't that kid anymore. He jerked off his hat and ran a hand through his hair.

The tape gun was in his truck. When he walked into the living room of the trailer a few minutes later, Beth had taken pictures off the walls. He glanced at the school pictures in cheap frames and shook his head. He'd always been surprised that his mom bought the school pictures each year and framed them.

"This is you when you were ten." Beth held up one of the photographs and smiled. "I remember that black eye."

"Yeah, me too."

He'd been fighting with Jackson Cooper at church. Tim had pulled them apart and given them both a sound talking-to. He still remembered being a scrawny kid looking up at Tim Cooper with that eye swelling shut and Tim seeming like the biggest man in the world. That's what he thought back then.

He'd wanted a dad real bad.

"Your mom has all of your school pictures."

Jeremy nodded and reached for one of the boxes and the tape gun. "Yeah, she did that. She always tried to dress us up that one day. And that year she tried to convince me to put makeup on my eye. I didn't."

"Of course you didn't."

He took the picture from her hands and set it down. He didn't want to think about that day and his mother telling him not to fight with Jackson. Because she'd known that Jackson was his brother. He grabbed newspaper and wrapped the picture.

"Was your mom always…" Beth bit down on her bottom lip and one shoulder lifted in a shrug. "I'm sorry."

"Beth, I'm thirty years old, not fifteen. Yeah, there are memories here, but I'm not a little boy who needs Band-Aids and lollipops. My mom is an alcoholic. And yeah, most of our lives she was drunk."

"But our mothers were friends in school."

"Yeah, they were. I think my mom was okay as a kid. She was raised by an aunt. But for some reason her aunt left when my mom turned about fifteen."

And then her high school boyfriend had been killed in a car accident.

Life hadn't been easy for Janie Hightree. She'd done her best to pass that legacy on to her kids, to keep the cycle going. He and Elise had pulled it together somehow, some way. He hadn't thought about it before, how they'd survived and actually done something with their lives.

Beth stopped asking questions. Jeremy grabbed a box and walked into the kitchen. He looked around and shook his head. She understood why. The room was a disaster. Dishes in the sink, empty bottles and cans, the trash overflowed and flies swarmed. The place had a stench worse than any barn she'd ever been in. It smelled more like the county landfill.

"I think the only way to deal with this mess is to

throw it all in the trash." He shuffled through cabinets and pulled out a box of trash bags.

Beth couldn't agree more.

"You know, I don't really need help. This is more than you expected and I really can do it alone."

Beth wrapped another photograph and placed it in the box. She walked into the tiny kitchen and pictured him there, a boy trying to take care of a mom and a little sister. As a teenager, even from the time he was eleven or twelve, he was always working odd jobs around town. Vera had put him to work washing dishes. Buck had hired him to clean stalls in exchange for riding lessons. Until Beth had been caught making eyes at him, and then he'd been sent packing.

She smiled, remembering him in that barn, faded jeans, worn-out boots and a threadbare T-shirt. She hadn't seen any of that. She'd seen a smile that set butterflies loose in her stomach and eyes that always looked deep into hers, as if he really cared what she had to say.

Even then he'd been different. He'd been two people—the tough kid and the sweet guy. Now he was the man who made her forget fear, forget all of those years thinking she wasn't worth anything.

And he was the man most likely to hurt her.

"I don't mind helping. I can even wash the dishes."

"No, these are going in the trash." He had already filled one garbage bag.

"What about the bedrooms?"

"There are two. Elise's room is cleaned out. Mom probably sold what she could, if there was anything to sell."

"And your mom's room?"

"More stuff to throw away. I went to the store the other day and bought new clothes for her to wear. The stuff in there isn't worth taking to her or giving away."

"So pack it all in garbage bags unless we find something worth keeping?"

He stopped stuffing trash into the bag. "There won't be anything worth keeping."

Okay, she knew when to let it go. She grabbed a trash bag and headed for the back of the trailer. The floor had weak spots that sagged and the paneled walls were dingy and stained by years of dust and nicotine. The bedroom at the end of the hall was a little bigger than the first, but not enough to count. A double mattress on a frame was pushed against one wall, the sheets a jumbled mess, an old quilt thrown over the whole mess. The closet was full of old housedresses, worn polyester pants and shirts.

The dresser held more of the same. The drawers didn't pull out straight and the top of the dresser was covered with books, papers and old dust collectors that had obviously done their "dust collecting" for years. She hated to throw away the figurines, thinking that at one time they had meant something to Janie Hightree.

As adamant as Jeremy was that it should all be thrown away, she wondered if Elise would feel the same way. These were her mother's few possessions. Beth grabbed an old shirt and dusted a few of the figurines. One was porcelain and dated. Had Janie kept it for a reason?

She placed it in a box and as she dusted, she added several more to the collection. Ten minutes later she was shoving clothes into a trash bag when booted footsteps came down the hall. She glanced toward the door as Jeremy walked into the room. He walked over to the box and picked up one of the figurines.

"What's this?"

Beth shoved the last of the clothes into the bag and pulled it closed.

"I don't know, I guess I just thought that Elise might feel differently. She might want some of these. Or perhaps you could put them in your mom's room."

Jeremy exhaled a sigh and put the figurine back in the box. He shook his head. "I don't really want that and it won't mean anything to Elise."

"Okay." She knew when to let it go. Sometimes.

Jeremy turned out to be the one who didn't let it go. He leaned against the dresser, his gaze traveling around the dingy, tiny room.

"Hard to believe this was her life." He shook his head and then looked up. "It could have been my life, or Elise's life. Somehow we escaped."

The moment stretched between them, silence hanging over the room. Beth stepped close. She put a hand on his cheek, felt the raspy five-o'clock stubble, and then his lips moved to brush across her palm. His hands moved to her hips.

Beth closed her eyes as his lips touched hers, sweet and gentle. She sighed into a kiss that moved her to new places, stronger places. He whispered her name at the end of the kiss and shook his head lightly.

"I'm not sure what we're doing here." He rested his cheek against hers and she wanted him to hold her close for a long time.

"I don't know either, but does it have to be wrong?"

And then she was cold and lonely because he moved to the doorway. How did she tell him that he changed things? He shifted her heart from broken and lonely to hopeful.

He made her feel safe.

How did she tell him something that important when he didn't know what they were doing here? She took that as her cue to leave.

Chapter Thirteen

Saturday night at the rodeo. That's what Jeremy needed after the week he'd had. He'd packed up his mom's trailer at the beginning of the week, gone to a planning and zoning meeting a couple of days later. He'd managed to steer clear of Beth because he needed time to get his head on straight.

He unlatched the back of his trailer and backed his horse out. The big gray stepped onto firm ground and lifted his head, ears alert as he took in the surroundings. The animal was so excited he was almost to the point of trembling.

The horse had needed this as much as Jeremy. They both loved the smell, the sounds and the action of the rodeo. He ran a hand down the light gray of the animal's neck and then led the horse to the side of the trailer to tie him while Jeremy got the saddle and bridle out of the tack room of the trailer.

"Hey, bro, how's it going?" Travis walked up, long-limbed and all energy. His dark-framed glasses didn't manage to give him a serious expression, not with the big grin on his face.

"Going good, Travis. What about you? You bullfighting tonight?"

"Nah, no bulls tonight. It's a ranch rodeo. What are you going to do?"

"I didn't know it was a ranch event." Teams of four or five guys doing events that were similar to work done on the ranch. Sorting calves, loading and simulated branding.

He hadn't really talked to Wyatt since a few guys started planning the rodeo. It was meant to be a way to raise funds for some of the folks in Dawson who were still struggling to get back to normal after the tornado. People had to be reminded that even though they were back to everyday life, quite a few of their neighbors were still in limbo. Several were living in campers. A few had moved to apartments in Grove. A couple of families were still at the church.

But the rodeo required a team and he didn't have one. He shoved his saddle back in the tack section of his trailer. So much for letting loose and burning energy tonight.

"You can take my spot on the Cooper Clan team," Travis said.

"No, that's okay." Jeremy brushed a hand down his horse's back. Travis got a little closer and eyed the gray gelding.

"Nice horse."

"Yeah, he's been real good for me."

Travis nodded. "Yeah, I think you should ride with Jackson, Reese and Dad. I'd give anything for a night off."

Travis glanced toward a trailer where a girl in dark jeans and a tank top was saddling a pretty bay mare.

"I bet you'd like a night off." Jeremy laughed at the younger man. But he got it. He'd also been searching for a face since he pulled into the rodeo grounds fifteen minutes earlier. He'd seen the Bradshaw trailer parked at the end of the row. So far he hadn't seen Beth. It was a ranch rodeo, but they'd still have barrels.

And then Jackson was strolling toward them. Jeremy shook his head. It was really about time to head for Tulsa.

"You don't have a team, do you?" Jackson Cooper spoke as he reached down to buckle his bright orange chaps. Yeah, that took some self-confidence. His shirt was orange, too. Kind of a peachy orange.

"No, I didn't realize it was ranch night." Okay, enough explaining. He needed to load his horse and leave.

Leave, as in straight back to Tulsa.

The lights flashed on around the arena. Jeremy untied his horse and Jackson was still standing there in his way.

"Where you going?" Jackson looked puzzled enough.

"Home. I'm not planning on running barrels and I'm not on a ranch team."

"I told him he could take my place on the Cooper Clan Team." Travis grinned big.

Jackson shrugged. "Works for me. Travis can't sort calves for nothing."

Because Travis couldn't stay in one place long enough to sort calves. It was easy. There were ten calves in one section and the team of riders had to sort the calves in order, bringing one calf at a time across the line to the other side of the arena. If a calf slipped over the line out of order, the team was done.

Travis liked constant motion and sitting on a horse long enough to keep calves from crossing a line probably wouldn't be his thing.

"If you take my place, they might really win." Travis jerked the number off his back and handed it to Jeremy. "Have at it, bro."

"Right." Jeremy looked at the number and he felt like he'd been picked by the cool guys to play on their ball team.

"Better get that horse saddled." Jackson slapped him on the back and walked away. "Glad you're one of us."

Jeremy tied his horse and reached for the bridle. And then he saw Beth heading his way, a country girl in faded jeans, a T-shirt and dark pink roper boots. He couldn't picture her in California, in a city. She belonged in Dawson.

He thought about that for a long moment and refused to think the same about himself.

"You riding?" She sat on the wheel well of the trailer and watched him saddle Pete, the horse.

"Yeah, I guess I'm riding with the Coopers."

"That's great."

He glanced her way before reaching under his horse to pull the girth strap tight. The horse stomped as the strap tightened under his belly.

"Yeah, I know, Pete." He lowered the stirrup back into place and then ducked under the horse's neck so that he was on the same side as Beth. "You riding tonight?"

"I'm trying that roan Dad bought." She pulled off her hat and smoothed her hair. "I guess it's quiet at your place since there are only a couple of families left in the church."

"Yeah, it's quiet." What else could he say?

"I should go take care of my horse." She stood up. Next to him she was tiny. He could imagine holding her close, lifting her in his arms. He couldn't imagine anyone striking her, ever.

Every time he looked at her this way, he wanted to run a finger over that scar on her face. He wanted to ask her if it still hurt, the deep-down-inside pain of the past.

She was healing.

He didn't want to hurt her all over again. He wasn't thinking about the church, he was thinking about him and that look in her eyes that said she wanted something more, something that lasted.

"I'm going to loosen Pete up a little and then find out what I'm supposed to do. I've watched ranch rodeo a few times but I'm as green as they get."

"You've been team roping a lot lately." She made the comment as she moved a few steps away from him.

"Yeah, with Dane Scott." Dane had a degree in engineering. The two of them were partners in the custom bike business. Dane didn't look like an engineer or a computer genius. He looked like a biker, the kind of guy that scared people when they met him in the dark.

He was the same guy who warned Jeremy that God wouldn't look too kindly on his plan to tear down Back Street. Jeremy figured he had Dane's prayers to thank for everything that had happened since he got to Dawson

"Well, good luck tonight." The look she gave him, all innocence and sweetness, was a lot like the look she'd given him years ago. It teased and tempted. It left him staring after her like his brains had been scrambled.

She fast-walked back to the Bradshaw trailer. It held four horses, tack and living quarters. The Bradshaws went big wherever they went.

He watched as she untied the dusky roan and mounted. He watched as she nudged the horse from a walk to a trot and then an easy lope away from the crowd.

"You going to admire the scenery or ride?" Jackson Cooper rode up on a big black gelding. The horse tossed his head and backed up, nervous energy already causing perspiration to soak his dark coat.

"Yeah, I'm riding. But don't forget that I've knocked that grin off your face before."

"And got a black eye for your trouble."

Good point.

Beth kept the gelding in control, holding the reins tight as the big animal trotted along the back of the rodeo grounds, bobbing his head up and down, wanting to break into a run. She eased him into a walk and turned him toward the trailer where Jason was tying his horse and talking to their dad and Lance. The other members of their team were standing at a nearby trailer.

As she rode up the driveway she thought about all the times in her life that this was normal. This was where she'd grown up and where she belonged. But Chance had convinced her that they could see the ocean, live a dream life and escape the country. Escaping the country had been what he wanted and she'd followed.

This would always be home. A dark, humid night with millions of stars sparkling in the sky, arena lights, hamburgers on a grill and the citizens of Dawson in the bleachers of the tiny rodeo arena that was Dawson's main form of entertainment—this was her life.

The horse beneath her jogged a little and pulled at the reins. She couldn't give him his head. He'd get to run soon enough. But he was raring to go. She loved the energy. After years of not riding, not barrel racing, she was glad to be back.

"Beth." Jenna Cameron rode up on a palomino mare. "You riding tonight?"

"I am." The two had been friends in school. They were closer now. They both suffered from mild post-traumatic stress disorder. Beth from years of abuse and being under Chance's control. Jenna had been injured in Iraq. She'd lost her leg from the knee down in a road-side bomb attack.

They had shared stories about fear, captivity, and being whole again. Beth smiled at her friend, who was one of the strongest women she knew.

"You know I'm going to beat you, right?" Jenna laughed, her smile bright. She had a lot to be happy about. She had Adam MacKenzie for a husband, twin boys and a baby girl.

Beth would have those things someday. She was starting to dream again. To hope.

"I'm willing to wager a steak dinner that you don't." Beth pulled the roan to a stop and Jenna stopped next to her. The palomino, creamy yellow in the bright lights, pawed at the ground.

"I'll see your steak dinner and raise you a cheese-cake."

"Great, now I'm too hungry to run barrels."

"That was my plan."

The announcer called for the invocation. The two women turned their horses toward the arena. Team Cooper rode past. Big men, big horses and lots of cowboy ego. Jeremy was with them, riding with his family. He nodded in her direction and she smiled.

"Interesting," Jenna murmured and then bowed her head as the prayer was said.

Beth waited until amen. "Nothing interesting, just a lot of imagination and speculation."

"Right." Jenna laughed. "Beth, how long have we been friends? I think you loved Jeremy even when you were twelve and he was teasing you in this very arena."

"That wasn't love, that was aggravation." But she couldn't help looking at him as Team Cooper was called and the men on horseback rode into the arena, discussing their strategy. At the far end of the arena a line had been drawn with flour. The calves to be sorted were on the other side of that line.

"Let's go see how they do." Jenna led the way. The two rode near the arena and watched. Jeremy went into the herd of calves, found number five and cut him from the herd. The calf ran across the line and Jeremy went back for calf six. The other riders kept the herd from crossing the line.

People were cheering. Jenna stood in her stirrups to

get a better view. And Beth realized she was holding her breath. He was a Cooper. Her heart picked up a few beats and she moved her horse closer.

A loud bang exploded in her ear. Beth's horse jumped forward. She grabbed at the reins, getting control as the animal started a series of bucks that jarred her teeth, her head, her neck. She heard Jenna yell for her to hang on.

That wasn't optional. It was hang on or land on the ground.

As the horse jerked forward, taking a few running leaps away from the arena, she heard her dad yell something about firecrackers.

The horse finally calmed down. He stopped, trembling, breathing hard. She stayed in the saddle, her own breath coming hard and fast as her heart slowly returned to a normal rhythm. She turned, and the horse took jerky steps, nervous, ears twitching.

"What happened?" Jeremy rode out of the arena straight toward her.

"Someone threw a firecracker," Jenna volunteered, her face a little pale.

Beth's dad led his horse up to hers. He grabbed the reins.

"Get off him."

"Dad, we're both fine."

"I'm not going to have a horse that can't be trusted."

"Someone threw a firecracker at his feet. You'd jump, too."

Buck Bradshaw's jaw worked, clenching and unclenching. "I wouldn't have put you on him if…"

"Dad, I'm a grown woman, not a child." She held the reins tight. The horse stood calmly, or as calmly as he could considering the arena, the lights, the crowd and the deafening noise that had startled them both out of ten years.

Jeremy rode up close to her. He opened his mouth and Beth raised a hand to stop him.

"If you're going to repeat what my dad just said, save your breath."

He grinned, luscious, heart-stopping and handsome. "I was going to tell you that was some pretty great rodeo."

"Funny." She swallowed and clenched the reins hard, not to hold the horse steady but to hide her trembling hands.

"I'm going to find the kids with those firecrackers," her dad grumbled and walked away. More like stormed. She watched him go and then turned back to Jeremy.

He leaned close. "You okay?"

"I'm good." She rode her horse in a tight circle that put a few feet between herself and Jeremy. "You did great out there tonight."

Couldn't she think of anything better than that? Shouldn't she tell him that she resented that he'd still tear down Back Street after everything the community had been through? Shouldn't she tell him she wouldn't let him break her heart?

Instead she'd complimented his riding skills.

"I need to cool this horse off before barrels. I can't stand taking a crazy horse into the arena," Beth said.

"Doesn't he have a name? You keep calling him 'horse.'" Jeremy reached down and patted the horse's neck.

"Yeah, his name is Trigger. How's that for sappy?"

"Cute. Call him Trig for short?"

"I guess."

And then he did the unexpected. But if a person always does the unexpected, shouldn't it become the expected? He rode up next to her and, before she could react, he was out of his saddle and sitting behind her. They'd done that a lot when they were kids riding in trail rides or just around the arena. He had one foot out of the stirrup and over her horse, pulling the two together and then sliding behind her saddle.

Trig hopped a little and then settled. Jeremy's arms were around her waist.

"What are you doing?" She glanced back but then faced forward again because he was close behind her, so close she could feel his warm breath against her neck.

This was why he'd kept all the girls talking when they were teenagers. Because he always knew what to do, what to say to make a girl fall.

"We're going to cool this horse down a little," he answered. He had the reins of his horse in his hand and the poor thing followed behind, ears back.

"I'm not sure this is a good idea."

She felt him shrug behind her. "Yeah, it probably isn't. But since when do we make the best decisions?"

"I know this is hard for you to believe, but I've been working on that."

"Are you saying I'm a bad decision?" He leaned close, his chin near her shoulder.

She inhaled and regretted it immediately, because he smelled so good. Her senses, the ones meant to derail bad choices and the ones that were tuned into the world around her, were all mixed up and colliding with a mess of other emotions.

The sharp scent of his cologne mixed with the mint of his gum. Combined with the rough feel of his hands on her arms and the warmth of his breath, she nearly came unraveled.

"Jeremy, what are we doing?"

He didn't answer for a second. "Beth, I'm not even sure."

Great, that made two of them. And she really needed for one of them to be sure of something.

"I think you should go."

He leaned back. His hands were on her waist and he rode loosely behind her. "And yet you're riding farther and farther from the arena."

Hmm, he had a point. And yet she kept going. Behind her he laughed and she smiled. "I'm going crazy. That has to be what is happening to me."

He reached and took the reins from her hands, trapping her between his arms, brushing his raspy cheek against her neck.

"I think crazy is okay once in a while, as long as you don't do something you regret." He kissed her on that spot beneath her ear and she closed her eyes for a brief second.

"Maybe."

"But I'm going to go ahead and take your advice and say goodbye. You do mean go as in get off your horse, not go back to Tulsa, right?"

"I think that's what I mean." She smiled back at him and he turned the reins back over to her. She pulled the horse to an easy halt next to his gray gelding and he slid a leg over, settling back into the saddle. Beth watched him ride away, then turned and rode back to the arena.

Two years ago she'd told herself she wouldn't travel this path again. She wouldn't open her heart up just to have it broken. Shouldn't it feel a little broken now?

Instead her heart felt as if the pieces were being put back together. By Jeremy Hightree.

And he had the ability to break it all over again. Either he'd leave, or he'd tear down the church. Both pointed to heartbreak.

So shouldn't she put her emotions in check and make a break from him before either of those two things happened?

Common sense was pointing to yes.

Chapter Fourteen

Monday after the rodeo Jeremy sat in his lawn chair looking at Back Street Church. They'd had services again yesterday. But by next week Dawson Community Church would be repaired and open once again.

Back Street would be forgotten. Again.

A truck pulled into the parking lot and pulled up next to his. Tim Cooper got out. Tim took his hat off and pulled out one of the spare lawn chairs. He shook it open and sat down.

"Nice day for sitting."

Jeremy nodded. "Yep."

Tim glanced across the road. "Saw you on that monster bike yesterday. Is it yours?"

"No, we built it for a customer. I'm hauling it to Tulsa tomorrow." The bike was already on the trailer attached to his truck.

Tim nodded. His gaze strayed to the church and he sighed. "It's been here a lot of years. I guess we did sort of let it go."

"Yeah, but it was here when people needed it."

"You mean after the tornado?"

Jeremy nodded. It didn't sit well with him, that the people in town were done with the building. It had served its purpose—again.

It had served a purpose when he was a kid. He didn't really feel like sharing that with Tim Cooper. It was good that he had stopped by and all, but they weren't ready for long discussions. But Jeremy had realized something about himself, and about this church.

The other day at his mom's trailer he'd caught himself wondering about how he and Elise had survived their childhood. Now he realized he hadn't survived on his own. Elise hadn't survived on her own. Man, it was hard to look at that church and think about tearing it down. He and his sister had survived because of this church and the people who had attended it.

He let out a sigh and shook his head. "I have a lot of memories tied to this building."

"Yeah." Tim cleared his throat. "I guess we all do. That's why I'm here. Joe Eldridge from the planning and zoning commission called me. He said they voted in your favor this morning."

"In *my* favor, huh?"

Tim let out a long sigh. "Yeah, you have your zoning. You can go ahead with the demolition of Back Street Church."

Months of working, fighting and waiting. Now that it was over, he didn't know what to think. The people of Dawson were done with Back Street. The last family had moved out of the shelter that morning. He could move forward with his plans.

"I guess I'm not going to tear it down." Jeremy glanced at Tim, his father. "I guess I thought it would make me feel better."

"Sometimes a man has crazy thoughts."

They both laughed. "Yeah, like dozing down a church. Like that dozer could really do the job."

"So, what are you going to do with it? And what about the business?"

"I don't know. I think I'm going to head back to Tulsa. And Back Street Church can go back to being a monument to the people in this town. Maybe they'll need it again someday."

"I hate to see you not build a shop here. There are people in town who need jobs."

Yeah, he knew that. He just didn't know if he could stay here any longer. Yesterday he'd watched Beth leave church with her dad and brother and he hadn't known how to deal with how he felt for her. He still didn't know what in the world name to put on it.

He'd never been in love before. He'd made a lot of bad choices and been in a lot of relationships that had meant nothing to him. He'd walked away from women who claimed they loved him and he hadn't felt a thing for them.

A few had told him he was breaking their hearts. So what was he going to do? Break Beth's heart? He'd rather cut off his right hand than hurt her.

"That tree over there looks like it got shook loose in the storm." Tim nodded in the direction of a soft maple that shouldn't have been planted so close to the building in soil as sandy as this.

"Yeah, I noticed that the other day. The roots are exposed and some of the leaves are starting to turn. It'll have to come down."

"I'm supposed to be picking up a gallon of milk from the convenience store. I just wanted to stop by and see how you're doing." Tim stood up. "I guess you'll be around?"

"I'll be around. I'm keeping this land."

"Right. You can take a guy out of Dawson but it's sure hard to keep him away."

"Something like that." Because Vera had the best pies in the state and people here were friends for life. And family.

He stood up and held his hand out to Tim Cooper. Tim took it and held it tight.

"Any man would be proud to call you son."

"I appreciate that."

Tim stood there for a long minute. "I guess we'd like for you to keep coming to our family dinners, even if you decide to leave us for Tulsa."

"I think I'd like that, sir."

"That's good."

Tim tipped his hat down, turned and walked away. Jeremy watched him get in his truck and then he turned back to that tree. Time for it to come down.

Beth had saddled up for a ride through the pasture but she'd changed her mind. She hadn't seen Jeremy, hadn't really talked to him since the rodeo. And that left a lot unsaid. She didn't even know what needed to be said at this point.

She knew that he had the go-ahead to demolish Back Street Church. She knew she couldn't stop him. She knew it would hurt. It would also hurt him.

It took her fifteen minutes to get to Back Street. As she got close she heard the dozer. Her heart tightened and she urged the horse forward, into a steady gallop.

They rounded the corner and the dozer was heading for the church.

She leaned and the horse stretched his legs and ate up the ground. As they raced across the lawn of the church she saw the dozer, saw Jeremy in the seat. She headed the horse toward the church, and positioned herself at the steps, between Jeremy and the building.

The dozer chugged to a stop.

"Beth, what in the world are you doing?" He leaned out, his hat shading his face.

"I'm stopping you from making the biggest mistake of your life."

He sat there, staring. And then he shook his head. "You like to think the best of me, don't you?"

She couldn't stop trembling. And seeing red didn't begin to describe how mad she was at him. "I do believe the best in you. I also know that I'm not going to let you do this."

"Beth, listen to me…" He jumped down from the dozer.

Beth remained on her horse. She backed the gelding up a couple of paces and made like she was a lot stronger than she felt. She wasn't backing down.

"You can get off that horse."

"No, I'm not going to. I'm going to stay here until you change your mind."

He snorted and shook his head. "You're the most stubborn female I've ever met."

With that, he walked away. Beth watched from her position in the saddle as he walked into his RV. All was quiet. The dozer was silent. The RV was silent. A few minutes later he walked out with a suitcase. He saluted and walked to his truck.

At the truck he stopped. "It's all yours, Beth. The paper is on the table in the RV. I'll be back in a few weeks to get my stuff. But try believing in someone. Just try believing that there are people out there who won't hurt you."

He tossed his suitcase in the back of the truck and drove away. Beth dismounted on shaky legs. She stood next to the gelding who turned to rub his head against her arm. She rubbed his face and leaned against him.

She waited for Jeremy to return. Years ago she had waited for Chance to return, but that had been different. She had awaited Chance's return with fear, wondering what he'd do next. She'd wait, wondering when he'd unlock the bathroom door and let her out. She'd waited, finally, for her chance to escape.

She'd come home on a bus, bruised, broken and afraid she'd never trust or love again.

As she sat on the church steps, her heart truly broke. She felt it tighten with pain and crumble into pieces. Her throat tightened with emotion and regret. Tears, cold and salty, coursed a trail down her cheeks. The horse grazed at the end of the reins, chomping as the bit clicked. She shouldn't let him do that. She should pull him up.

Instead she sat on the steps and waited.

A truck finally did come down Back Street. Jason turned into the parking lot and got out. Her brother walked across the lawn with an easy gait, a smile on his face.

"What are you doing over here?" He studied her face and she turned away.

"Trying to decide if my first mistake was trusting him or falling in love with him. I'm trying to decide if my second mistake was pushing him from my life or if that was the best thing to do."

"Gotcha." He sat down next to her. "So, where is he?"

"Packed a suitcase and left. He said the church is mine."

"Interesting. But he left?"

She nodded and a fresh wave of tears and pain swept over her. She pulled up the collar of her shirt and wiped her eyes. She was so done with crying, so done with feeling empty.

Jason got up. "I'll be right back."

She nodded and continued to cry. The horse pulled on the reins. She pulled him back and tied him to the handrail. His ears flicked this way and that but then went back to show his displeasure because he'd been enjoying a patch of clover.

Jason returned, a paper in his hand. "He signed it over to you. Do what you want with it, he says. And there's a P.S."

"What?"

Jason grimaced as he read the note and then looked at her. He shook his head. She wanted him to read it. She wanted him to get it over with. "Jason, please?"

"He was only going to knock down the tree. But..." Jason shrugged and handed her the note. "You read it."

She took the paper and held it tight. The words wavered and her eyes overflowed. "He was only knocking down that tree before it fell over and hit the church. And he didn't feel like defending himself." Good going, Beth. She closed her eyes. "I didn't give him a chance to explain."

Jason grinned at that little revelation and cleared his throat. "You were hardheaded?"

"It does run in the family." She should have trusted him. He'd never given her a reason not to trust. "I just automatically think the worst. I don't want to be that person."

Jason sat back down. "You're not that person. And Jeremy Hightree has a lot to work through. Maybe he's trying to work through his feelings, or yours."

"Mine?"

Jason leaned back and gave her a long look. "I'm not sure if he's ever had anyone love him the way you do. That's a lot for a guy to deal with."

She started to deny that she loved Jeremy, but that was a pointless argument. She wouldn't be sitting there on the church steps bawling like a baby if she didn't love him.

"What do I do?"

"Give him time, Beth. He'll be back."

She glanced back over her shoulder at the church. The paper was in her hand, telling her that it was hers. Her church.

"What do I do with the church?"

Jason shrugged. "I don't know. You offered to buy it before. What would you have done with it if you'd bought it?"

The ridiculous situation dawned on her and she started to laugh. She laughed until she cried, but not sad tears. "Who gets a church from a guy? Other women get roses, jewelry, candlelight, romantic dinners. I get a church."

"Alyson always tells me not to buy her flowers because they wilt. She'd rather have plants for the flower garden."

"I have a church." She sighed and stood up, facing the building. The horse walked up behind her, pushing his head against her shoulder. "I'm not sure what to do with it."

Jason had stood. He untied the horse from the handrail and slipped the reigns over the animal's head. "Pray about it, Beth. I can't help but think God had a hand in bringing this all about. This church has sat here empty for the better part of the last ten years. It's time for it to be used and you're the person to decide how."

She nodded and slipped her left foot into the stirrup. As she swung into the saddle her gaze went to the building. Again she sighed, because it was too much for one day. Jeremy leaving, the church, it settled heavy on her heart.

"I'll pray about it." She held the reins loosely in her right hand and smiled at her brother. "Thank you."

As she turned the gelding toward home she heard a basketball bouncing on pavement. Two boys were walking across the parking lot, heading toward the basketball nets Jeremy had put up.

Beth smiled and watched the two kids as they started a game of horse. A few minutes later another boy arrived with his skateboard.

As she headed home, plans began to whirl through her mind. She didn't have to urge the horse forward; he was ready to get home. They seemed to be in the same mood, both a little lighter and a little more free.

Chapter Fifteen

Jeremy walked through his Tulsa dealership studying the way the manager had arranged motorcycles. It was late June and the weather was great. Several customers milled around, probably dreaming of the perfect day and a bike to ride country roads. Yeah, he knew that dream. He'd spent the last couple of weeks, since he'd left Dawson, taking advantage of as many days like that as he could.

Today the bikes looked perfect. They were polished until the paint gleamed and the chrome could reflect images. In the far corner were a few custom bikes, for customers who wanted something out of the ordinary.

"Jer, you got a minute?" Dane Scott walked out of his office, a big guy with bleached hair, a goatee and a heart of gold. He was raising his sister's two kids because she'd never been able to get her act together.

"I have a minute and we have a fresh cup of coffee." Jeremy headed toward his own office and knew that Dane would meet him there with his mug that said THIS IS THE DAY THE LORD HAS MADE. Jeremy kind of laughed because the mug and the man didn't match, not unless you knew Dane.

Dane walked into the office, holey jeans and a short sleeved button-down shirt, loose tie around his neck. He kicked the door shut, poured himself a cup of coffee and sat down. Jeremy stood behind his desk, waiting, because he had a feeling this was going to be good.

"Get out of here." Dane's words were soft, easy, and pretty stinking determined.

"What?"

"You're driving us all crazy. I don't know who you left behind in Dawson, but man, I've never seen you like this. And it's starting to get on my nerves."

"I don't know what you're talking about." Jeremy loosened his own tie and sat down behind his desk. The big chair was leather and soft. It fit him like a glove. This office fit him. It got under his skin that Dane would tell him to leave his own business.

Dane leaned forward, muscled arms folded on the desk. He grinned big. "Buddy, I've known you for years. We team rope together. We play golf together. We chase women together. We're confirmed bachelors and we love it."

"Right, that's us." Jeremy leaned back in the chair and worked real hard at casual.

"Yeah, it *was* us. When was the last time we went out? When was the last time you had a date? Have you taken Paula out since you got back from Dawson?"

Paula. A woman busy with her career and not interested in long-term relationships. She was lively conversation at dinner and even played golf.

"No, because we've both been busy."

"No busier than usual. As a friend, I'm telling you to

take care of whatever is eating at you. I think we both know that it has something to do with Dawson and that church you didn't tear down."

"I told you, we're building on the five acres where my mom's trailer used to sit."

"Right, that's a good location, not in a neighborhood. Perfect. What happened to the church?" Dane grinned and leaned back in this chair.

"You prayed for me and my plans fell apart. Thanks for that." He sighed and shook his head. "I mean it, thank you."

"Not a problem. God and I were looking out for you, keeping you from making a huge mistake. And now I'm telling you, don't make another decision you're going to regret. You have good people here. You have a manager who makes sure each location is on target. You don't have to live in this dealership."

"This is my business."

"And you're going to chase away the customers if you keep stomping around frowning. Look, playing the field is all good if it's what you want. But if you stop wanting that, if you start thinking of picket fences and baby cribs, then it's time to let it go."

Jeremy laughed at that image. "Right, that's me, a picket fence and baby crib kind of guy."

Dane shrugged. "Kids aren't all bad. I mean, girls, yeah, they're kind of a pain when they get all moody and emotional, but they have moments when you see the person they're going to be someday."

"Right." Jeremy stood up and stretched. He looked out a window that faced a busy street. In the distance he could see the downtown businesses, the tall buildings reaching up. He could watch planes take off.

He loved his place on the outskirts of Tulsa.

He had planned on living his life here, away from Dawson. He had planned on never settling down. Man, he had a lot of plans. And lately, none of the plans fit. His plans felt like cheap boots, a little tight, uncomfortable and ready to be kicked off.

The day he'd left Dawson he'd felt good about leaving. He'd been saving Beth from being hurt by him. He didn't do long-term relationships and he cared about her too much to play that game with her.

Today walking away felt like the worst thing he'd ever done, not the most chivalrous.

"So?" Dane still sat in the chair watching him, a cheesy grin on his face. "Do you need to go buy a ring?"

Jeremy glanced down at his friend. He thought a lot of things about Dane right then. Some of it wasn't too PG. And then he thought that not many people would sit him down and force him to look at his life the way Dane could.

"Yeah, I need to buy a ring." Because he realized then that he'd played the field and never fallen in love because he'd been in love for years. With Bethlehem Bradshaw.

Back Street Church Community Center. Beth stood back and watched as Ryder Johnson helped her brother put the sign in place at the edge of the lawn. She smiled at them, and at the newly painted building. The church was no longer empty and forgotten.

It was now a place for the people of Dawson to gather for family reunions or special events. It was a shelter. It was a place for kids to hang out. Twice a week after school snacks would be served and homework help provided. There were basketball hoops, volleyball nets and a homemade baseball field.

The community had something worthwhile, because of Jeremy Hightree. She glanced across the street at the empty barn, the forgotten foundation of the home he'd given up on. Only one family had left town after the tornado. One family, and Jeremy.

It hurt to think about that day, about watching him drive away.

"Kind of empty over there without his livestock." Jason walked up, work gloves in his hand. He shoved the gloves into the front pocket of his jeans.

"Yeah, a little." She smiled up at her brother. "I should have trusted him more."

"Maybe. But sometimes we go by what we see even when we know that faith is evidence of things unseen."

She nodded and wiped at eyes that overflowed far too easily these days. She had always loved Jeremy in some little way. She'd loved him as a kid because he'd been hurting and tough. She'd loved him as a teenager because he'd been that guy that always knew the right thing to say, the right way to smile and flirt.

As an adult? She loved him because he made her feel strong, not afraid. Because he made her heart feel a little less fragile. She loved him.

And because she hadn't trusted, he was gone.

"I keep praying that he'll come back," Beth admitted. "I want him to see what I've done with the church."

Jason laughed. "Yeah, that's the only reason you want him back."

"I want to apologize for doubting him," she admitted.

It wouldn't do any good to admit she was in love with Jeremy. He wasn't a man looking for a wife and a home to settle down in.

"Right. You keep telling yourself that, sis." He hugged her. "I have to get home. Ryder already left. Andie called and said he had to get home and help her corral the twins."

Beth nodded and her heart did a little dance thinking about those twin baby girls of Andie's and Ryder's. "I'm going to make sure the lights are off inside the church and lock up."

"Will you be okay here alone?"

She looked at the church and nodded. "I'm fine here."

He was asking because of Chance. But Chance had left again. His dad had driven up to the ranch and apologized for his son. He'd told Beth that Chance was moving to Oregon. He'd met a girl.

If only Beth could warn the poor thing. Online Chance was probably a perfect man. He was handsome, educated, wealthy. He was everything a woman wanted, online.

Online he could be whoever he wanted to be. In person he was a different story.

"I'll see you tomorrow." Jason kissed the top of her head.

"Give Alyson my love."

Jason nodded and walked away. She watched him leave and then she headed for the church. She remembered that day weeks ago when she'd walked through the doors of Back Street and felt lost and alone.

It was no longer a rejected, forgotten building. The inside glowed with promise. The windows were clean and cobwebs were gone. The kitchen in the basement had been remodeled. One of the rooms was now a nursery and the pantry held emergency supplies.

She stood in the sanctuary and said a silent "thank you."

"Bethlehem Bradshaw, I'll tell on you."

The voice was velvety soft and a catch of emotion punctuated the words. She didn't turn, couldn't. Her heart froze and then hurried to catch up.

Finally she turned. He stood in the doorway, a cowboy in faded jeans, a T-shirt and worn boots. His hat was cocked to the side. When he smiled her world tilted a little.

"What are you doing here?"

He took a few steps forward. "I had some unfinished business here. By the way, I like what you've done with the place."

She bit down on her bottom lip and waited to hear what his unfinished business was. Her gaze slid down, to the Bible in his right hand. Her mother's Bible.

Should she say she missed him? Or maybe ask if he wanted the church back? She should ask about his mother or if it was true that he was building his business where his mother's trailer had been.

Instead she stood there unable to say anything at all. He took a few more steps, his smile so sweet she wanted to melt into his arms and ask him to never let her go.

Chapter Sixteen

Jeremy didn't want to rush this. For two days he'd been thinking about what he'd say. He'd thought about it when he put his place in Tulsa up for sale. He'd thought about it when he bought the townhouse that would be his place to crash when he checked on his business in Tulsa.

He'd thought about it when he went shopping.

Now he had it all in his head, and even in his heart, but he didn't want to rush it. What if he was wrong and she wasn't interested? What if he was thinking that his bachelor days were over and she had no intention of settling down with a guy like him? A thousand "what-ifs" played through his mind, scaring the daylights out of him.

All of a sudden his plans were tossed out the window when one of his surprises came wobbling into the church, fat-bellied and short-legged. He knew it was there before he saw it because Beth's gaze dropped and her mouth opened and then turned to a smile.

"Aw," she cooed.

He looked back and he was right. There it was, wobbling down the aisle. He reached to grab the German shepherd pup before it peed on the newly polished floors of the church. It struggled a little and then went to town licking his face.

"It's adorable."

He handed the puppy over to her. "I saw him in a pet store window and he looked like a guy that needed a bigger home."

She took the puppy that looked like a bear cub and held him close. His licking went into overdrive. Jeremy watched, and he felt as if he'd done at least one thing right. Who needed a bouquet of flowers when they had a puppy? He'd actually thought about the flowers, but the ones at the convenience store in Dawson were pretty wilted and brown.

So now what? He'd stalled for at least three minutes. Beth looked up and her eyes sparkled a little. Was she glad to see him, or was it the puppy that put that smile on her face? For a guy who had dated his fair share of women he realized he really knew very little about them.

"Beth, can we talk?"

She raised her face. The puppy squirmed in her arms, still trying to zero in on her cheeks.

"Of course we can." She bit down on her bottom lip. "Jeremy, you haven't changed your mind, have you?"

"My mind?"

"About the church. I mean, you left the letter and I ran with it. There were kids here every day, playing basketball, riding skateboards. I realized that there are churches in Dawson, but nowhere for the kids to hang out. People complain the teenagers in town are causing problems. I just thought if they had somewhere to go…"

He took her free hand and lead her out of the building. "Beth, I'm not taking the church from you. I gave it to you. It's yours to do whatever you wanted with."

"Thank you."

"I have other unfinished business." He led her down the steps. He didn't know where they were going, but somewhere.

"Unfinished business?"

He kept walking. There was a bench under one of the big trees in the front lawn of the church. He led her there but they didn't sit down. Beth put the puppy down and it walked around the bench and then plopped down in the grass.

Unfinished business. She was far more than that. He held up the Bible that had been her mother's. Her gaze drifted from his face to the book he held. She shook her head.

"I don't understand. You didn't have to bring it back."

He smiled, and he could no longer resist touching her. He touched her cheek and then slid his hand back. His fingers tangled in the silky strands of dark hair. Beth's eyes lowered and she moved closer.

"I missed you," he whispered, and he couldn't imagine ever being away from her again.

Beth opened her eyes to those words. Her hands rested on his arms, as if they had a mind of their own. He had backed away, though.

She had missed him, too. But she didn't want to say it, not yet. She didn't want to go where she might get hurt. Living near the lake, she'd always been taught not to jump into the water unless you knew what was beneath the surface. It was good advice. And in this case, she didn't know, not yet.

Jeremy held up her mother's Bible. He flipped through the pages and handed it to her, open to the back section.

"I've been reading and I found something that I think might be a problem." Jeremy pointed to the page he'd opened to.

She shook her head because she didn't get it. This wasn't what she wanted, a discussion about her mother's Bible. She wanted to know that he was back to stay. She wanted to hear him say something about them.

"Jeremy, I don't understand."

He grinned, his eyes sparkling with that old mischief and humor that she'd known since childhood.

"Look at this page, Beth. The page where weddings and births are recorded."

"Right?"

"It isn't filled out."

She looked down, wanting to understand because he obviously wanted her to get it.

"No, it isn't." She sighed and touched the pages. She should write Jason and Alyson's wedding details on these pages.

And then she saw what he was trying to point out to her. The page was marked with the blue ribbon that her mother had used to keep the place where she was reading. Tied to the end of the ribbon was a ring.

Beth's breath caught and she didn't know what to do. Crying seemed good, or the laughter that bubbled up. Her heart couldn't catch up with Jeremy.

"Beth, your mother never got the chance to record weddings." He grinned. "Or the births of new children.

I think we should take care of that for her. I think we should put our names on this page. Jeremy Hightree and Bethlehem Bradshaw, married…" He touched her cheek again and this time his lips touched hers and he held her close, as if he never meant to let her go. "I don't know, what day do you think we should write on the date line? It's getting close to the end of June. Maybe August. Or September?"

Her words refused to spill out in a way that made sense. She had an answer, she really did. He was smiling at her.

"Beth, I'm putting my heart on the line here." He spoke softly, his mouth close to hers. "Do I need to kiss you again?"

That made perfect sense. She nodded and he captured her mouth with his, a persuasive kiss that explored what her heart had been trying to tell her for weeks. He pulled her close and she wrapped her arms around his neck.

She wanted this, forever. She pulled him closer and he kissed her more. And then he stepped back. He took off his hat and sighed.

"Bethlehem Bradshaw, will you please marry me?"

She nodded and tears flowed down her cheeks. "I will marry you, Jeremy. Today, if you want."

He smiled that big cowboy smile of his and he lifted her up off the ground and twirled her. The puppy barked a fierce puppy bark and Jeremy set her back on the ground.

"I love you." He kissed her again and she tried to whisper that she loved him back. She had always loved him and she always would.

Epilogue

Two months later

Bethlehem Bradshaw stood at the front of Back Street Church. Wyatt Johnson held her mother's Bible. Behind him was the pulpit her great-grandfather had built. Her family sat on the pew where she'd always sat with her mother. And instead of sitting behind her, Jeremy Hightree stood next to her. He smiled down at her, and she couldn't believe this gorgeous man in his Western tuxedo was going to be her husband.

That morning they had recorded their wedding in her mother's Bible. Jeremy Hightree married Bethlehem Bradshaw, August 28, a Sunday afternoon. Witnessed by family and friends. Her father gave her away. Her brother was the best man. Her sisters-in-law, Alyson and Elise, were her bridesmaids.

Wyatt Johnson smiled at the two of them. "I now pronounce you husband and wife. You may kiss the bride."

The church erupted in applause. Jeremy pulled her close. His ring was on her hand, joined with her mother's wedding band. He smiled as he whispered that he loved her. The kiss was sweet and easy and another round of applause cheered them on as he held her in his arms. And then he lifted her and carried her out of the church.

Next year they would hopefully fill in the next page in the family registry, the page for births. She closed her eyes and dreamed about a family with the man holding her close, carrying her out the door to a stretch SUV limousine.

Jeremy and Bethlehem Hightree. She now knew how it felt to be loved by someone strong. She had engraved the words from her mother's journal on the wedding page in the Bible.

Love will happen. Life will happen. Don't rush through the days, savor them. Love someone strong.

* * * * *

Dear Reader,

Welcome back to Dawson! Readers have emailed me on occasion to ask when certain characters will get their story, their romance. One of the characters people have asked about is Beth Bradshaw, sister to Jason Bradshaw in *The Cowboy's Courtship*.

I was only too happy to give Beth a story. When she first showed up in Dawson, I realized she'd been through a lot and she was going to need a special man, someone strong and caring. Along came Jeremy Hightree, a cowboy who'd left town years ago and is back only to tear down one of Beth's most beloved childhood memories.

Jeremy and Beth join forces when a tornado hits Dawson and Back Street Church is needed as a shelter. Thrown together, they find love and healing. I hope you'll enjoy their story.

Brenda Minton

QUESTIONS FOR DISCUSSION

1. Beth Bradshaw faces her fears and her past simultaneously. The past is the first thing she deals with. When she returns to Back Street Church, what emotions does she encounter?

2. How does God use returning to the church to bring change to Beth's life?

3. Beth has a very real fear that stems from an abusive relationship. How does that tie into confronting her past and Jeremy?

4. Jeremy Hightree wants to tear down Back Street Church. What are his reasons?

5. How does God use Jeremy's desire to tear down the church as a way to heal his past?

6. Jeremy's mom ties directly into his anger and yet he cares for her and about her. How does God change our hearts so that we can be angry and yet not hurt those we're angry with?

7. The Bible says to be angry and sin not. How does that apply to Jeremy and even to our own lives?

8. The tornado was an act of nature, but how did God use it in the lives of the people in this story?

9. Tim Cooper cheated on his wife, Angie. They're still together and their marriage appears strong.

How do people face such an obstacle and move on with their lives, keeping their family intact?

10. Beth left a man who abused her for several years. What kept her in the relationship? What did it take for her to finally walk away?

11. Victims often suffer from PTSD (post-traumatic stress disorder). How does this change Beth's life and how she deals with life?

12. Beth's father was angry with Back Street Church. Why is it that when faced with a crisis he blamed God? Was it easier to blame God, to have something or someone to be angry with rather than accept what was happening to his wife?

13. Beth and Jeremy have been through similar situations and both have had their faith tested. Both had a crisis of faith that changed their lives. How did they renew their faith?

14. Beth pushed to save Back Street Church. Why was saving the church, a building, so important to her?

15. Why was it important to Jeremy to see it gone?

16. Why did Jeremy give up on tearing down the church?

17. When did Jeremy realize he loved Beth?

INSPIRATIONAL

Inspirational romances to warm your heart & soul.

Love Inspired

TITLES AVAILABLE NEXT MONTH

Available June 28, 2011

THE FARMER NEXT DOOR
Brides of Amish Country
Patricia Davids

THE NANNY'S HOMECOMING
Rocky Mountain Heirs
Linda Goodnight

A FAMILY FOR SUMMER
Love For All Seasons
Lois Richer

PHOEBE'S GROOM
Email Order Brides
Deb Kastner

THE DADDY SURPRISE
Ginny Aiken

MOM IN THE MAKING
Kit Wilkinson

LICNM0611

REQUEST YOUR FREE BOOKS!

2 FREE INSPIRATIONAL NOVELS
PLUS 2
FREE
MYSTERY GIFTS

Love Inspired.

Read on for a preview of the first book in the heartwarming new ROCKY MOUNTAIN HEIRS *series,* THE NANNY'S HOMECOMING *by Linda Goodnight, on sale in July from Love Inspired.*

Gabe Wesson was a desperate man.

Inside the Cowboy Café, a hodgepodge of various other townsfolk gathered at the counter for homemade pie and socializing. Gabe sat on a stool, his toddler son, A.J., on his knee.

He'd discovered that if a man wanted to know anything in the town of Clayton, Colorado, the Cowboy Café was the place. Today, what he needed more than anything was a nanny.

He'd found Clayton, a sleepy community time had forgotten. With an abandoned railroad track slicing through town and an equally abandoned silver mine perched in the nearby hills, the town was just about dead.

It was the just-about that had brought Gabe to town. He had a knack for sniffing out near-dead businesses and resurrecting them.

But unless he found a nanny for A.J. soon, he would be forced to move back to Denver.

On the stool next to Gabe, a cowboy-type angled a fork toward the street. A white hearse crept past. "They're planting old George today."

"Cody Jameson, show some respect," red-haired Erin Fields, the surprisingly young café owner, said. "This town wouldn't exist without George Clayton and his family. Speaking ill of the dead doesn't seem right. His grandkids are here for the funeral and *they're* good people. Brooke Clayton came in yesterday. That girl is still sweet as that cherry pie."

Gabe listened with interest, gleaning the facts and the undercurrents. He wondered if George's heirs knew he'd sold the mine to an outsider.

Gabe and A.J. stood and pushed out into the summer sun as the last of the funeral cars crawled by. A pretty woman with wavy blond hair gazed bleakly through the passenger window. Something in her expression touched a chord in him. He knew he was staring but couldn't seem to help himself. The woman looked up. Their eyes met and held. Sensation prickled Gabe's skin.

The car rolled on past and she was gone. But the vision of Brooke Clayton's sad blue eyes stayed behind.

George Clayton's will stipulates that his six grandchildren must move back to their tiny hometown for a year in order to gain their inheritance. With her life in shambles, Brooke Clayton is the first to comply. Could she be the answer to Gabe's prayers?

*Look for THE NANNY'S HOMECOMING
by Linda Goodnight available in July
wherever books are sold.*

SHLIEXP0711